12-73 " 4 "

WD

High Fly
to Center

by BILL J. CAROL

Steck-Vaughn Company
An Intext Publisher
Austin, Texas

With affection and gratitude
this book is dedicated to
Susan

Library of Congress Cataloging
in Publication Data
Knott, Bill, 1927–
  High fly to center—by Bill J. Carol.
  SUMMARY: Determined not to miss playing on
his Little League team, Mickey Ortega runs away
from his parents' vacation cabin and tries to make
his way home.
  [1. Baseball—Stories]   I. Title.
PZ7.K755Hg   [Fic]   70–176067
ISBN 0–8114–7737–1

ISBN 0–8114–7737–1
Library of Congress Catalog Card Number 70–176067

1

MY NAME IS Mickey Ortega. You may have read my
other book, the one that told about Ollie and me and
the trouble I had last year getting started as a Little
League baseball player. I'm older now, and I can
write much better, at least I hope I can. I was just a
kid then, anyway. Now I can tell you about my second season playing for the Tigers. It was some season,
believe me.

I guess my trouble really began the first game, even
though it didn't seem like trouble at the time. We
were playing the Giants, and they got off to a real fine
start against us. In fact, they scored seven runs in the
first inning.

And it wasn't all Paul Norwood's fault either. The
first batter slashed a mean one right at the mound. It

skipped past Paul's glove and headed for me in center field. I put one knee down and waited for it—forgetting what I had learned the year before, so of course, the ball hopped over my shoulder and headed for the fence. By the time I mailed the ball back to the infield, the batter was standing on third base, grinning out at me.

Paul was a little upset and walked the next batter.

Then he calmed down and struck out the next fellow on three sizzling fast ones. But the batter after that sent a line shot over third base. Bob Lenney trapped the ball in the left field corner and threw it in. Two runs scored, and the batter reached second.

Now Paul was really unhappy. He threw four wide pitches to the next batter. Two men on. After that a couple of batters in a row singled, and poor Paul was taken out.

Jimmy Kingston went in to pitch. His first pitch was wild and in the dirt. His second pitch hit the batter and bounced high off his shoulder. That loaded the bases. Mr. Farber called time and went out to talk to Jimmy. This settled Jimmy down some, and he struck the next batter out, sending three balls over the plate so fast that the batter just seemed to be closing his eyes and swinging.

Two outs.

Then came a low drive into center. I ran in and tried to make a shoestring catch to end the misery, but just missed. By the time Bob Lenney recovered the ball at the base of a wooden fence in deep center, the sacks were as clean as a whistle.

Jimmy struck the next batter out, and I started in. I didn't really *want* to go in to the bench, you understand. After that miserable performance in center field, I wasn't anxious to meet Coach Farber's eyes—or Paul Norwood's either, for that matter. Still, I had no other place to go. I sure couldn't stay in the outfield. But the closer I got to the bench, the worse I felt. Sometimes I think this is the worst part of baseball—coming in to the bench after booting the ball around.

"Hi, Mickey," said Paul Norwood, looking glumly up at me as I reached the bench. "Join the funeral."

"You guys want to bury me?" I asked.

"Hey! Snap out of it!" called Mr. Farber. He was actually smiling at us. "This game isn't over yet. We've got lots of time to get those runs back. Let's go!"

Jimmy Kingston was moving toward the batter's box. He glanced back at us. "That's right, you guys! Besides, there's a scout from the Astros in the stands!"

"A scout!" said Bob Lenney. "From the Astros?"

"Sure," said Sandy, looking back at the packed bleachers. "This is my big chance!"

"Hold out for a big bonus, Sandy," said Bill Tebo. "At least a hundred thousand."

"At least," said Sandy, still trying to pick out the scout.

Just then the crack of Jimmy's bat brought us all around and up on our feet. The ball he had just clobbered was on its way, skipping past the shortstop and into left field. Jimmy made the turn for second, kind of casual like, then suddenly shifted into high and slid into second just ahead of the throw.

"That's the way to hustle!" called Coach Farber, clapping his hands. He turned to the bench. "Let's have some coaches on first and third!"

I darted out to the third-base coach's box. It was a funny thing. I wasn't sure if Jimmy Kingston was kidding or not; but as I crossed the grass, I could almost feel the eyes of that scout on my back.

It turned out I was all of a sudden a very busy third-base coach. Bob Lenney singled. Terry doubled. I sent Jimmy and Bob in to score; and when Jack Tilson stepped into the batter's box, I left the coach's box and hustled toward the on-deck circle.

Tilson walked, and with two men on, I stepped up

4

to bat. The first pitch to me was as straight as a baseline and not really too fast—for a called strike. I stepped out of the batter's box and gave myself a talking to for not swinging at it.

"What's the matter?" asked the Giants' catcher. "Having a nervous breakdown?"

"That's right," I told the kid grinning out at me through the bars of his mask. I noticed he had a front tooth missing. "That pitcher of yours is fast!" I told him. "Are you sure he's not too old for Little League ball?"

"Don't worry. He won't hurt you. He's got great control. Just don't figure to get any hits."

"Okay, you two," said the umpire, "let's play ball."

I stepped back into the batter's box, hoping that I had convinced the catcher to ask his pitcher for another pitch just like the one I let go by. The pitcher looked in for his sign, nodded, went into his windup, and pitched. Sure enough. It was a carbon copy of that last pitch—straight and true and right over the heart of the plate, belt high. It came up as big as a grapefruit. I had dug in, and now I swung from my heels. The bat connected solidly. It felt great—the way it does when you really get hold of one—and I followed through all

5

the way around, dropped my bat, and made a dash for first.

The rest of the team was screaming at me, and the crowd in the stands was really letting go, too. I looked up as I raced down the line and caught sight of the ball. It was still rising. The center fielder was drifting back, farther and farther. And then he came to the fence and stopped, turned, and watched the ball drop over.

A homerun! The first one I'd ever hit! Even in practice I had never hit a ball like that before! As I rounded the bases I felt kind of giddy. I had to remind myself to step on each base. And then I slapped my foot down on home plate and charged into the crowd of players waiting for me. Boy, did they pound me!

Well, anyway, that made it seven to five. We needed two more runs to even things up, and we got them, plus one more for good measure.

As I trotted back to my position, I felt great. I mean, I had come in feeling like a bum—and here I was going back to center field a hero. Boy, what a hit! I was glowing and thinking of that Astro scout in the stands.

The first batter up for the Giants swung wildly on three of Jimmy's fastest pitches and went back to his bench, talking to himself. I relaxed. Jimmy was doing fine. Then he walked the next batter. Man on first.

I pounded my glove and yelled, "Hey in there! Get two!"

The batter swung, connected, and I saw the ball leave the bat, heading for deep center. It was going to be a tough one, I realized as I started to run. I kept my eye on it and raced back as fast as I could. Just in time I saw the fence and pulled up. The ball was coming down now, and I was almost under it. The fence was holding me back, so I reached out over the fence, holding my glove up like a cup, and let the ball land in it. Just like that. Honest. It was as if I knew all along that I couldn't miss it.

I bounced off the fence and gunned a throw to Jack Tilson on first. He doubled up the runner, and I started in.

In the third I came up with two men on, two outs. I didn't offer at the first pitch, and it was a called strike. To tell the truth, it went by so fast that by the time I figured it was a good pitch, the catcher was throwing it back. But on the next pitch I was lucky.

The pitcher tried to get smart and threw a slow one that came in right over the plate. I swung from the heels and clocked it. On one bounce it was past the left fielder, and I pulled up on third with a triple.

In the top of the sixth, after the Giants had loaded the bases with two outs, the batter sent a mean line drive over second base. I was off at the crack of the bat, racing in full tilt. The ball was sinking fast, but I kept on coming, reached down, and felt the ball burrow into my glove like something alive—and stick there.

The game was over, my best game in a long time; I felt great.

As I was leaving the park later with Terry, someone called out my name. I turned. Coach Farber was standing with an older man, and Jimmy Kingston was with him. The older fellow had broad shoulders and was dressed in a baggy, gray business suit with his sport shirt open at the neck.

His face was what I noticed right away. It had been tanned a dark nut-brown and had wrinkles in it. His big jaw was thrust way out, and his eyes were sharp and clear. When he smiled at me as I approached, it was as if I were looking into the face of a young man, despite the sprinkling of white hair at the temples and the wrinkles.

When I reached him, I stuck out my hand. He shook it, and I was impressed with the strength in his grip and also with the calluses on the palm along the base of the fingers like the ones I got every spring from swinging the bat.

"This is Jim Martin, Mickey," said Mr. Farber. "A great third baseman in his time with the Boston Red Sox."

"You mean he's the scout with the Astros? The one Jimmy told us about?"

"Right, Mickey," said Jim Martin. "I'm scouting now for the Astro ball club."

"Wow!" said Terry. "We didn't know whether or not to believe there was a scout in the stands."

"I did," I said. "I believed it."

"And you played well, Mickey," said Jim Martin. "Have you boys considered the possibility that you might play in the Majors someday?"

"The Majors!" I said.

"Wow!" said Jimmy.

"It's a possibility," said Jim Martin, smiling at us for the way we jumped at the idea. "Ballplayers grow old, you know. There's always room for strong young arms and legs and keen batting eyes. You seem to have all three in abundance, Mickey. You, too, Jimmy."

Mr. Farber broke in then. "Now don't you boys go home and tell your parents to pack your bags—not just yet at any rate."

I looked at Jimmy and swallowed. I wouldn't do anything as silly as that, of course—but still—the way Jim Martin talked . . . and the way he looked at us!

On the way home I had trouble keeping my feet on the ground. I could hardly believe it. A big league scout—someone who had once played with the Boston Red Sox—had just suggested that I might be able to play Major League baseball myself someday.

I guess you might say that that was the beginning of my trouble. I had just caught the Major League virus!

2

DAD CLEARED HIS throat loudly and leaned toward me.

"I *said,* pass the butter!" he almost shouted at me.

"Oh."

I picked up the butter plate and passed it to him.

"Thanks. Glad to have you back with us."

"You were miles away, dear," said my mother. She looked concerned. "Are you worried about something?"

"He's got a girl friend," piped Audrey, a toothy grin on her freckled face. She held her fork straight up, and she was talking with her mouth full.

"Shut up, squirt," I told her. "I don't have a girl friend."

"Well, now that you're back with us," said my

father, "I would like for you to tell me when you're going to get to work on that lawn. You were supposed to do it as soon as you got home from school."

"I had to practice."

"No. You had to do the lawn."

"I'll do it after supper."

"Fine."

I went back to my chops and mashed potatoes and was surprised to find them stone cold.

After supper I went out to the garage, started the lawnmower, and began to mow the front lawn. But I couldn't get out of my head the words of that baseball scout. The Major Leagues! Me—up to bat with the television announcer following my every move while the crowd roared. I could feel the bright sun on my red-and-white home uniform, for I was now playing for the Boston Red Sox. Watching the pitcher carefully, I was squeezing the handle of the bat until it almost squeaked. I was holding it high and back over my right ear, an unorthodox stance that would soon make me famous.

The pitcher was fast, blinding fast, but I was ready for him. I saw the ball leave his hand, and I strode forward smoothly, brought my 36-ounce bat around with swift, lethal control and connected solidly. The crowd was on its feet, its exultant roar shaking the ground. I tossed aside the bat, glanced up to watch the ball begin its drift into the center field bleacher seats, and then I started for first.

Not until I reached third base did I doff my cap to the crowd. This was my third homerun in as many games. As I crossed the plate, I reached out with both hands to grasp those of my teammates waiting for me . . .

"Mickey!"

Startled, I stopped the lawnmower and looked around. The mower was on the sidewalk, and my father was standing beside me, his face red. He must have been yelling for some time, trying to get my attention.

"What's the matter, Dad?"

"What are you *doing?*"

"I am mowing the lawn."

"On the *sidewalk?*"

"Well, I . . ."

"And look behind you, if you don't mind. Where you've just been."

I turned around. There was a neat swath cutting across Mom's flower garden. My heart sank.

"What's the matter with you, Mickey?"

13

"I was thinking," I said.

"About *what?*"

"About . . . about playing on the Boston Red Sox someday."

"The Red Sox?"

"That's right."

He nodded, then shook his head. "Well, okay, Mickey. But first, what say you concentrate on just mowing the lawn."

"Sure, Dad."

He started off back to the house, then turned and came back. "Keep thinking about the Major Leagues, Son. But for goodness sake, remember that all of that business is a long way off yet. And when you finish, you can go to practice, okay?"

"Okay, Dad. Thanks."

I went back to the mowing. In fact, I got so involved in it that I couldn't hear my folks when they began calling to me from the porch. At last I heard them above the roar of the motor and turned. My father was standing with his hands on his hips, and my mother was waving something in her hand.

I turned off the mower and looked again at what Mom was waving. It was yellow—a small envelope. And then I remembered. My report card! I had forgotten to give it to them when I got home.

14

"Hurry up and get over here!" called my father. His voice was heavy. My heart dropped down to my toes. He had seen my grades, I could tell.

I started for the porch.

"You didn't show us your report card, Mickey," Mom said when I got to the house. She sounded disappointed, as if I had forgotten on purpose to show it to them. "It dropped out of your jacket when I started to hang it up."

"I forgot," I said.

"You forgot!" roared my father. "Well, I guess I would, too, if I had to bring home a report card like that one. Get in here, young man."

"I haven't finished mowing the lawn yet," I protested. "And baseball practice begins in a few minutes. Remember, you said I could go to practice as soon as I finished."

"Practice! Baseball practice! Is that really *all* you think of?" he demanded. "I said get in here!"

I scooted past him and went into the kitchen. Whenever we have discussions—about discipline, chores, or the way I treat my sister, things like that —we end up sitting around the kitchen table. So I sat in my usual seat, and Dad sat in his, right across from

15

me. He seemed really upset. But Mom was a lot quieter. She gets that way whenever Dad starts shouting, I guess to help calm both Dad and me.

Dad had taken my report card from Mom. Now he was holding it between his thumb and forefinger, as if it were something dead, if you know what I mean. Boy, I would have liked to have seen a report card of *his*. But of course I didn't say that. I just swallowed and waited for the blast.

"According to this card," my father began ominously, "you are not doing so well—not well at all!"

"It's just the warning report card, Dad," I said.

"Well, it's some warning all right."

"I know," I said. "I'll just have to work harder, I guess."

"You guess!"

My mother spoke up then, her voice troubled. "Mickey, you've only got a few weeks before school lets out. You know that, don't you?"

"Sure, Mom."

"Well, did you have any homework for tonight?"

I nodded.

"Where is it?"

"Upstairs."

"What subjects?" my father asked.

"Arithmetic and social studies."

16

"Arithmetic is your worst subject," he said, glancing down at the report card. "You're getting 60 in it. That's all. Sixty. And that's failure."

"I'll bring that up, Dad."

"How? By playing baseball?"

"I'll do better on my tests," I said lamely, feeling kind of desperate all of a sudden.

"You're not doing so well in social studies, either," my father reminded me.

"How come? I passed it."

"You passed it just by the skin of your teeth. You're right on the fence. One single point lower and you would have failed. Is that good enough for you —just passing?"

"No," I said. My voice sounded kind of faint.

"I think," suggested my mother gently, "that you'd better get upstairs right now, Mickey, and get busy on your homework."

"But, Mom! I'll be late for practice!"

"Never mind practice!" my father bellowed. "Forget that ball team! Your schoolwork comes first."

"You can go as soon as you finish your homework, Mickey," said my mother.

"But first you finish that lawn," my father added.

By this time my head was spinning. I couldn't believe it. It was a disaster—a four-alarm disaster.

17

"But I can do my homework afterwards," I pleaded, "when I get back from practice. It won't take me long to do it."

"You heard your mother," my father said ominously. "Now get outside and finish the lawn; then get upstairs and finish your homework. After that, we'll see about baseball practice."

I looked at Mom. She looked straight at me, her lips together, a slight frown on her small face. She wouldn't contradict Dad. When it came to Audrey and me, they always stuck together.

"But I'll miss most of practice," I said.

"You'll miss *all* of practice if you sit here and argue with us," my father reminded me. "And furthermore, if you don't pass every subject—and that includes arithmetic—you won't enjoy our vacation this summer, because we won't bother to get that canoe you wanted us to get."

I sagged. What could I do? They had all the cards. I got up and went back outside to finish mowing the lawn.

Somehow—I don't know how for sure—Audrey found out what was up. She has a kind of instinct for knowing when I'm in trouble. Honest. Anyway, the first thing I knew she was standing in front of me, a big grin on her face. I kept the lawnmower going toward her. She hopped aside just in time.

"I saw your report card!" she yelled. "It was awful! You can't even add two and two."

Let me say right here that I know I shouldn't have gotten so angry. Audrey is much nicer than she was last year. She has pigtails and freckles, but her nose doesn't look like a tiny button anymore, and her knees aren't so knobby. And sometimes when I say things to her I shouldn't, instead of sticking her tongue out at me, she kind of pulls back and looks at me—as if she were trying to figure out if I really meant it. Other times her eyes get all bright and shiny, and I have to hurry and tell her I was only kidding.

But this time I was truly upset, so I lost my temper. I turned the mower around and went straight for her. She held her ground for a second or two, then turned and ran. That did it. I kept right after her.

She tried to duck aside, but I was really going by this time. She screeched and ducked around a tree. As she did so, her foot caught on a root, and she went tumbling down on the other side of it. I pulled up beside the tree and crouched behind the mower, waiting for her to come up from behind it. And then I saw my folks hurrying down the porch steps.

I turned off the mower. As soon as I did, I heard Audrey. She was really howling.

"What happened?" I cried, running around to the other side of the tree.

But as soon as she saw me, she ducked back. Both Mom and Dad were almost to the tree by this time, and I knew they could see how Audrey was flinching away from me.

"Come on," I said to Audrey, trying to calm her down. "What's wrong? I'm not going to hurt you. I was only kidding."

Then Mom stepped between us and lifted Audrey to her feet. That was when I saw Audrey's knee. It was all bloody where she had fallen onto something sharp. I looked down. There was a piece of a broken bottle lying in among the tree's roots.

Mom was trying to stop the bleeding with a hand-kerchief, but she wasn't having much luck; so Dad picked Audrey up in his arms and began to carry her toward the house. Audrey was not crying so much now, and Dad looked back at me.

"Leave that mower where it is," he said, "and get up to your room. I'll finish the lawn. And don't leave the room until I see you. Now go!"

20

I knew enough not to argue with him now. Boy, I was really going to get it.

I did my homework in my room while I waited, and for most of the time I could hear my father mowing the lawn. For the first time in my life, I guess, I found myself wishing I were out there doing the mowing. When I finished my homework, the lawnmower was still going, so I went back over my arithmetic and found a couple of errors.

At last the mower stopped. I put down my pencil, closed my arithmetic book, and shoved it over to a corner of my desk—and waited. It was getting later every minute, and practice was well under way by this time.

And maybe that scout was there, watching.

There was a sharp knock on my door, and that warned me. As my father pushed the door open, I got up from the desk.

"Hi, Dad."

He nodded curtly and shut the door behind him.

"How's Audrey?"

"She'll be all right. But that was some gash she suffered."

"Gee, I'm sorry, Dad. I didn't mean it."

21

"Sit down, Mickey," Dad said. "You're not going anywhere tonight."

"But, Dad!"

"You're lucky Audrey didn't cut herself a lot more seriously than she did. What's the matter with you, Mickey? Taking out your temper on a little girl like that—and your own sister, at that?"

"I didn't mean to . . . I was just kidding. You know that."

He shook his head like he couldn't believe it. "Just kidding! Chasing her with a lawnmower! Do you know how dangerous those things are? When are you going to grow up?"

"I'm sorry, Dad. Really. I didn't mean to hurt Audrey."

"Well, you did—and I'm going to have to punish you, Mickey. You're grounded for the rest of the week. It'll be good for you. You'll come home, get your homework done, and find something around the house to do." He looked around my room.

My heart sank, and I dived to pick up some socks from the floor and a T-shirt I had forgotten to put in the hamper. But it was no use. The room was a mess. A real mess. I hadn't cleaned it in a couple of days.

"That's right," Dad said. "Maybe you could even clean up this room. It needs it. And the garage. I've told you more than once that I want that garage cleaned up."

"And the cellar?" I muttered in complete despair. "Don't forget the cellar."

"That's right," Dad said grimly. The cellar, too."

"But, Dad. You've forgotten. What about the team? I've *got* to practice."

"The only thing you've got to do, Mickey, is do your work at home and at school. And obey your parents and leave off picking on your sister. Is that clear?"

"But if I don't show up for practice, Mr. Farber will think . . ."

"It doesn't matter what Mr. Farber thinks, Mickey. It's what your mother and I think. *That's* what matters."

"But . . ."

"Is that *clear,* Mickey?"

I gave up and nodded.

"All right then." My father got to his feet and glanced over the pile of books on the corner of my desk. "Your homework finished?"

"Yes, Dad."

"Good. Why don't you try studying that social studies text until bedtime. Seems to me you just read the chapters assigned. You never think to read a few chapters ahead, I'll bet."

I nodded, sheepishly.

"Well, try it. You'll be surprised at how much it helps."

"Is that what you did, Dad?"

He smiled then for the first time since he entered my room. "It's what I should have done, Mickey."

That remark took some of the sting off what was happening to me, but it still left me with real trouble. When my father closed the door behind him, I shook my head. The trouble was he didn't really understand about baseball and me, for I had just about decided that this was it. If I were going to play Major League baseball for a living, why did I need to read social studies books and study arithmetic?

I sat for a while looking at the closed door. Then I picked up my glove and threw it across the room as hard as I could. But it just thumped against the wall and fell to the floor without any real enthusiasm. For a moment I debated throwing the social studies book next, but then I decided I was already in enough trouble.

Light footsteps approached the door, and I heard Audrey's knock. I was about to shout at her to go away, to leave me alone; but before I could get it out, she opened the door and walked in.

"Close the door," I said. I tried to sound dramatic. "Close the door on my prison."

She turned after closing the door and looked at me. She was still puffy under the eyes from crying, and there was a large bandage around her knee. Right away I felt sorry for what I had done. But I didn't want her to know it, of course.

"Did you come up here to gloat?" I asked.

Right away her eyes filled up. "I'm sorry, Mickey," she wailed. "I didn't mean to get you into trouble. I didn't think Dad would ground you for a whole week. Honest."

"Oh, that's all right," I said as quickly as I could to stop her crying. "It wasn't you anyway. It was my school grades. They are really the reason he's grounding me. Hey, how's your knee anyway?"

She brightened at once. "It's not too deep a cut, although Mom almost took me to the hospital. And did it bleed!"

"Did it hurt?"

"Sure. But I didn't cry about that. That wasn't what made me cry. Mickey, you scared me. You really did. I mean, you looked so fierce, like you really were going to run over me with that lawn-mower!"

"I'm . . . sorry, Audrey. I wasn't thinking. I just wanted to scare you is all."

"Well, honest, you *really* did." She smiled brightly then. It seemed as if—now that she could look back on it in safety—she actually admired me for the ferocious way I came at her.

I wanted to reach out then and pat her on the head. But, of course, I did no such thing. "Well, thanks for coming up," I said. "I've got some studying to do now."

She nodded and went to the door. As she opened it, she looked back. "I'm sorry, Mickey."

Then she was gone.

I sighed and got to my feet and went over to my desk. I wasn't so angry anymore. I picked up the social studies book and began to read the next chapter—the one we hadn't come to yet. Of course, whenever I thought of what the rest of the team was doing at that moment, I felt an ache inside me. And I wanted to play ball so badly I could almost taste it.

But I kept on reading.

3

WELL, I DIDN'T play as much ball after that as I would have liked. I had to hit the books instead of the ball. But it wasn't such a bad idea, because now I was really beginning to understand what was happening in my classes. Besides, I have always liked to read, and my reading speed is good. The arithmetic took a little more effort than social studies, but that also improved as I paid better attention in class. I kept at it and caught up surprisingly fast.

As a result my grades improved, and my graduation into the seventh grade took place on schedule. From then on I was able to concentrate all my attention on baseball. That scout hadn't shown up at our games the last couple of weeks—and for this I was glad, since I hadn't been to many of them.

A week after school let out, we were playing the Bears on our home field. Both of us had gone scoreless until the top of the third when Paul Norwood made one pitch a little too fat. I saw the ball leave his hand and followed it over the plate. It was belt high. I braced myself as the batter swung. He connected solidly. The ball began to rise swiftly, getting larger every second. I knew I was really going to have to fly to catch up with it.

I was running full tilt the moment the ball left the bat, pulling hard, taking long strides. But I could sort of feel the fence getting closer. Even so, I did not dare take my eyes off the ball. It was starting to come down. Though I was still not under it, I was fairly certain now that I could catch it.

But how close was the fence? I glanced at it and found I had plenty of room. But when I looked back up for the ball, I saw I was out of line. I was no longer under it. Frantically, I changed direction, reached up, and saw the ball glance off the heel of my glove. I chased the distance for the ball, snatched it up, and heaved it in to Bill Tebo, racing out from second base to take the relay. But Bill's throw to the plate was long overdue; the batter had scored hours before.

I stood by the fence and punched my glove in frustration. After that fine run, I had missed the ball.

I knew why, of course. I had taken my eye off the ball to see where the fence was. I shouldn't have been so cautious.

"Nice try!" called Lenney from left field. But I just nodded. He didn't know what I knew, perhaps. I should have caught that ball.

The next batter hit a line drive to Bill Tebo to end the inning.

"That was a nice run," said Mr. Farber when I reached the bench. "You almost caught it."

"I should have," I said. "I took my eye off the ball to look for the fence."

Mr. Farber smiled. "I was wondering if you knew what happened. Anyway, nice try."

I nodded and moved past him to the bench and slumped down beside Terry. "Too bad," said Terry. "You almost caught it."

I glanced over my shoulder. My father was in the stands back of our bench. He was sitting four rows back. I caught his eye, and he nodded.

Then I saw someone else—that big league scout!

"Hey," I said to Terry, "that Astro scout is watching."

"So what," grinned Terry. "He's not going to offer

29

you a contract until the game's over. Settle down."

"After that muff I just made in center, he won't offer me anything . . . ever."

We went out one-two-three that inning, and I picked up my glove and trotted out to center field, my knees suddenly weak. I could just feel that scout's eyes on me.

Fortunately, no one hit anything out to me that inning, and Paul had little trouble getting the Bears out. In the bottom of the fourth, I was the third batter. Lawson struck out. Tilson lifted a soft fly to the right fielder, and I stepped up and strung the count out to three-and-two, then went fishing for a wide curve for the third strike and the final out.

In the fifth inning, we failed to score, although we loaded the bases.

In the top of the sixth, Paul walked the first batter to face him. Mr. Farber came out to settle him down. But the next batter doubled down the left field line. Then Jimmy Kingston fielded a hot grounder to the left of second and threw the ball into the stands. Paul Norwood slammed his glove down onto the ground in an impressive display of temperament.

With two runs already in, no one out, and a man on second, I could hardly blame him. I pounded my glove and yelled encouragement. I told him it was all right. We'd get those runs back. He turned and looked bleakly out at me. It was as if he were a soldier on high ground whom everyone was shooting at and someone had just told him there was no war on.

The next batter swung and sent a line drive to my left. I was off at the crack of the bat. The ball was low and sinking fast, but what we needed now was an out, not another single. So I went for it. I reached out and down, felt the ball slam snugly into my glove, pulled up swiftly, and fired the ball into third. Sandy Amaro flagged it down with one foot on the bag to double up the runner.

The next batter sent a high pop into the air over second, and Jimmy Kingston gathered it in for the final out of the inning.

This time my head was up as I trotted in to the bench.

"Okay, here we go, fellows!" shouted Coach Farber. "We can pull this one out. All we need is a few runs. Let's go. Everybody hits!"

Terry Lawson hit a routine grounder to shortstop. But when the shortstop went to throw the ball, he lost control of it, and Terry was safe. This error upset the pitcher somewhat. He walked Jack Tilson on four straight pitches. As the tall gangling first baseman tossed his bat aside, I left the on-deck circle and started for the plate.

"Come on, Mickey!" Terry called from second base. "Knock me in. You can do it."

Others behind me on the bench said about the same thing as I dug in. But I was nervous, very nervous. The palms of my hands were sweating. I had to wipe them on my pants' legs. And I kept feeling the eyes of that scout behind me in the stands. Now was the time I was going to have to make up for that high fly ball I had missed earlier.

I let the first pitch go for a called strike. The fellows on the bench told me to forget it, that I should wait for one I liked. Trouble was, I would like to have swung at that pitch. It had been belt high and right over the plate.

I stepped back out of the batter's box, bent down, and grabbed a handful of dirt.

"Welcome back," said the catcher when I returned to the batter's box. "Feel any better now?"

I didn't answer.

The next pitch came just as fast as the first one; but it looked outside, so I didn't offer at it.

"Strike!" called the umpire.

Oh, boy. I looked at the umpire, but said nothing.

Then I stepped out of the batter's box and glanced over at my bench.

"Pick out a good one, Mickey boy!" David Parisien yelled. "You can do it!"

I stepped back in and pulled my bat back. The pitcher wound up and let fly. This one looked good. I swung. The ball was inside, though, and I was lucky to get a piece of it. I fouled it into the dirt.

"That's the way to cut, Mickey!" Mr. Farber yelled.

I readied myself for the next pitch. It came in a little outside, but it looked good to me, and I swung —hard. I caught the ball on the fat part of the bat and sent it on a line over second base. The center fielder was playing me to pull the ball to the left; and as I lit out for first, I saw him digging hard to overtake the ball and cut it off.

But I knew he wasn't going to be able to do that, so I made the turn at first without slowing down, crossed second going flat out, then headed for third. Bill Tebo was coaching third, and he motioned me to stay on my feet. I pulled up with a triple and two runs knocked in! I felt great, but we still needed another run to tie it.

Sandy was up.

"Let's go, Sandy!" I called. "Just a little bingle."

33

And that's just what he produced, as he stepped into a high pitch and slammed it into center. I trotted home with a tying run, and a moment later Bill Tebo doubled him home to win the game.

It was a sweet victory, and as we gathered around Mr. Farber to cheer the Bears, I couldn't help looking around to see if that scout were still in the stands. When we finished our cheer for the losers, Terry and I started back toward the stands where my father was waiting for us.

To my surprise I saw my father close to the scout, who was evidently heading toward Mr. Farber. As the scout passed my father, he turned to him and said something. I guess he introduced himself, because he stuck out his hand, and then he and my father shook hands.

As I reached them, I heard the scout speaking. "Yes sir, a real fine game." Then he looked at me. "Looks like you might have a Major Leaguer on your hands some day, Mr. Ortega. This boy can really come back."

"I sure messed up that fly ball," I said, feeling my face blush.

"But you made up for it with that double play. You played that low liner perfectly. You didn't hesitate a moment. You started right in and kept coming."

Mr. Farber joined us then. "Don't give Mickey too

much credit," he said smiling, "or he'll get too big for his britches."

"Good ballplayers never get that big," the scout said. Then he and Mr. Farber said good-bye to us and walked off. My father looked down at me.

"I could almost swear you're blushing, Mickey," he said.

"Maybe," I said. "Maybe."

He laughed. "Fine game. You certainly *have* become a good ballplayer. Too bad Ollie couldn't have been here tonight."

I nodded.

Ollie was a former Minor Leaguer who had visited our town the year before. He and my father had taught me all they could about playing ball. But Ollie was not around this year. He was living on his Minor League baseball pension and kept moving—from bus terminal to bus terminal—as he followed the sun south and played ball wherever he could. I imagined he was in some small town right now, probably helping some other kid play ball. He sure helped me.

After we left Terry at his house, my father cleared his throat nervously. "It looks like the team is really going to miss you."

35

I was surprised at that. "What do you mean, Dad? Why will they miss me?"

"I just learned today, Mickey. Frank Jackson—that retired mechanic who used to run the garage before I bought it—well, he's back from Florida now, and he has agreed to take over the garage for me for three weeks starting Monday. That means we can go on that vacation to the mountains I've been talking about for so long."

"But I thought we were going at the end of summer, Dad. Late in August, after the Little League season was over."

"That's what I thought too, Mickey. But Frank's the one calling the shots—and he wants to take over now. Seems he could use the money for a boat he's planning to buy in Florida. You know I can't just let anyone take over the garage for three weeks. It has to be someone like Frank who knows what he's doing."

"But Dad! That means I'll have to leave the team for three *weeks* . . . that's six games!"

He smiled. "Oh, they'll survive without you, Mickey. Like I said, they'll miss you. But no one player is indispensable."

We were crossing a street then. I was so upset, I stopped right in the middle of it. "But I'll miss them!

I need the practice. I might even lose my position to someone else. And I've got to practice every day and play all the time if I'm going to be a Major Leaguer!"

My father looked around nervously. "This is no place to argue—in the middle of the street."

I finished crossing the street. "But, Dad, this is *important* to me! It's a matter of my whole future!"

He laughed. "Stop it, Mickey. It's just Little League baseball. Two years ago you didn't even know what a baseball was. Bring some books to the camp and read. You're leaning way over the other way now. All you did before was read. Now all you want to do is play baseball."

"But you don't understand!" I stopped walking and looked up at him. He looked around to see if anyone were watching us. "You just don't understand at all. Someday I'm going to be a Major League ballplayer."

We started walking again, and Dad's face grew serious. "Look, Mickey, I think it's fine you want to play ball professionally someday. But that's a long way off. Not only that, but . . . well, you've just got to consider the facts that you might not be good enough—no matter how hard you try."

That really hurt. After all, Dad had just seen how I had helped pull that game out. And he'd heard what

37

Jim Martin had said to me. "Well, maybe you don't think I could do it, Dad," I told him, "but I do. And so does that scout."

"Mickey," Dad said, smiling sadly—looking like he was really beginning to feel sorry for me—"what makes you think that every little boy who likes to play ball can grow up to be a Major Leaguer? It's as if you were reading one of your books. Make-believe. Fiction. By the way, Mickey, how good a ballplayer was Ollie?"

"He was great."

"He could hit anything we could pitch. And he could catch anything within reach—and then some—in the outfield. Right?"

I nodded.

"And yet, Mickey, he never made it to the Major Leagues. The top Minors were as high as he could get. Triple A ball. And now look at him—a drifter, a diesel mechanic working for a bus line, playing ball in small towns for whatever ball club or group will have him. Is that the kind of life you want?"

"*He's* happy, Dad."

"But is that all you want for yourself?"

We were at the house by this time. I started up the porch steps. I knew what Dad wanted me to say, and I didn't want to make him angry. I still hoped I could convince him to let me stay behind when the family took the vacation.

"No, Dad," I said. "I guess that's not what I want for myself."

He slapped me affectionately on the back, and we went inside.

4

THE BOAT SHOP was filled with all kinds of boats—sailboats, flat-bottoms, canoes, speedboats, and, in one adjoining shed I happened to glance into, cabin cruisers. The place even smelled of boats—a kind of glue and varnish smell. The fiberglass boats were all colors: pink, red, white, and on one little speedboat, a deep rich orange.

I followed Dad over to where most of the canoes were. They were all up on one end, leaning against the wall, their flaring bottoms facing out. Dad stopped in front of one and tapped the gleaming aluminum lightly with the back of his fingernails.

"I still like this aluminum," he said. "No upkeep. No painting, no sanding—and the hulls will take quite a beating."

A short, stocky man wearing a baseball cap and a white T-shirt with an anchor emblazoned on it approached us. "Can I help you?" he asked Dad, taking the unlighted stump of a cigar out of his mouth.

"Yes," Dad said. "I'm looking for a canoe. How much are your aluminum ones?"

"Depends. What length are you interested in? This one is a fifteen footer. One-hundred and ninety-eight dollars. It's on sale. She's a fine canoe for that price."

This was the third night Dad and I had been looking around for canoes, and this was the best price yet. Most of the canoes had been well over two-hundred dollars. I looked at Dad. He seemed interested and looked at the bottom of the canoe.

"That's a good price," he said.

The salesman smiled and shrugged. "Like I said, mister. This is a sale."

My father looked back at the canoe. "Okay," he said. "We'll take it." He turned and winked at me, then looked back at the salesman. "Unless you're having a sale on boat racks, I can't take it home tonight."

The salesman smiled. "Okay," he said. "We're having a sale on boat racks. I can let you have a fine pair for nine-ninety-eight. And you'll need paddles and cushions, too. Right this way."

Dad nudged me, and we followed the salesman. I could tell Dad was feeling pretty good about buying the canoe. The trouble was he thought I felt as excited as he did. And I did try to act as if I were. But I just couldn't go along with how he felt—even though when we had talked about it this winter, I had really been excited about the idea.

On the drive home, with the new canoe securely tied to our new boat rack and the backseat piled high with cushions, paddles, life jackets, and rope, my father glanced at me.

"What's the matter, Mickey?"

"What do you mean, Dad?"

"You're awfully quiet."

I shrugged.

"I thought you'd be quite pleased about buying a canoe. Don't you like this one?"

"Sure, it's all right. That was a good price."

"Yes, it was."

We rode for a while in silence. It got deeper and deeper. I tried to think of something to say, but I couldn't. Then my father spoke.

"Mickey, you're not one bit excited about this, are you?" He turned onto the street. "You're faking it.

Perhaps I should have brought Audrey along. She wanted to go, you know."

"I wouldn't have minded Audrey tagging along."

"I know that, but I thought we should do this together, the men of the family."

I shrugged. "Well, we did. We bought ourselves a canoe. Mission accomplished." I tried to sound light, but I guess the way I said it didn't go over very well.

Dad swung into our driveway without a word, his face suddenly hard.

As soon as the car rolled to a stop in the driveway, Audrey came charging out of the kitchen door. She took one wide-eyed look at the aluminum canoe on top of our car and began hopping about on the grass like a crazy rabbit. And she kept clapping her hands.

She was still jumping up and down when I got out of the car, and she was saying, "Oh, boy! Oh, boy!" over and over again.

"Do you like it?" Dad asked her, coming around the front of the car, a big grin on his face.

"Do I like it!" Audrey cried. "It's beautiful! It's the most beautiful canoe in the whole world!"

Dad bent over and swept her up in his arms.

43

"That's my girl," he said. Then he turned to me. "Let's take it off the roof for now, Mickey, and bring it into the garage. We won't be leaving until Saturday morning—since you have that game Friday night."

I nodded, and the two of us set to work. Audrey was so exicted she couldn't keep away from us. She seemed to be everywhere, trying to help, looking for ropes to pull, things to carry, and ways to be helpful.

Finally, when I was lifting my end of the canoe down and stepped back, I almost tripped over her.

"Get out of my way, will you!" I yelled.

Audrey stepped back, too quickly—and tripped over one of the white-painted stones along our driveway. As she landed on the grass—a look on her face close to tears—I saw the way Dad looked at me.

He was upset. But he didn't say anything as he continued to back into the garage with the canoe. When we had set it down against the wall, I straightened up and looked at him.

"Can I speak to you for a minute, Dad?" I asked.

"What is it?" He wiped beads of perspiration off his forehead with the back of his arm.

"Terry's mother and father said they wouldn't mind if I stayed with them while you were away on your vacation, Dad."

"While I was on my vacation, Mickey?"

44

"Yes, Dad."

He looked at me for a long moment, his face getting grim. His heavy, square chin actually seemed to grow bigger. Then he shook his head, slowly but firmly. "This is not *my* vacation. This is the family's vacation. We're all going *together.* This is a family, Mickey, not a collection of individuals. And you're a part of that family. No matter how you cut it, that's the way it's going to be. Do you understand?"

"Yes, Dad."

"Good. Now help me with those paddles and the tackle and the rest of the gear."

When we left the garage, Audrey was standing on the grass where she had fallen earlier, watching us. I could tell from the look on her face that she knew something was up. Still she was fairly bursting with excitement about the canoe and the upcoming vacation.

And as I watched her, I wished suddenly that I could have shared it.

I saw I had a big lead on first, but Bill Tebo hit the ball sharply to the shortstop who then flipped the ball toward second base to start a double play. I increased my speed and then launched myself, feetfirst through

45

the air at second base—and the second baseman. He was reaching out for the ball just as I slammed into him.

My plastic hat went flying. My face seemed to explode past a forest of legs, and when I came to rest finally, my feet were lying across the bag. The second baseman was on one knee in the grass, the ball still rolling away from him toward the pitcher's mound.

The pitcher ran over and scooped up the ball. I turned quickly to see if I was all right. The shortstop was racing over to take the pitcher's throw if I was off the bag. But I wasn't. I reached back and grabbed the base and then got to my feet. The pitcher threw the ball anyway, and the shortstop tagged me, but the umpire just shook his head.

All hands were safe as a result of my taking out the second baseman. But I had hit him hard, so I called time and asked the kid if I had hurt him. He shook his head and grinned shakily.

"That's okay," he said. "Nice slide. I should have been watching for it."

It was the last inning, and we were behind twenty-one to twenty-two. You're right. It wasn't exactly a pitcher's duel. But I represented the tying run; and since we had never been ahead in the whole game, I had a feeling that if we ever did tie this game up, we'd go right on to win.

46

Dave Parisien was the next batter. He took an outside pitch for a ball.

"That's the way to look them over," I called to him.

Dave swung on the next pitch and connected solidly. I was off as soon as the bat met the ball. As I cut toward third, the ball carried just over my head on its way into left field. Jack Tilson was coaching on third. He waved me around to score, and I really began to dig hard. I swung way out past the foul line and then aimed myself at home plate. I saw the catcher crouching for the ball. But with a sudden burst of speed, I was past him and across the plate with the tying run.

A moment later, Paul Norwood sent a long blast into center. But it was hauled down by the Giants' center fielder for the third out.

Neither team was able to get anything going until the top of the ninth when the Giants loaded the bases with only one out. Still, for some crazy reason, I felt sure we were going to win—even with the bases loaded and the count three and two on the Giants' best hitter.

Paul pitched. The batter swung. I was off as soon as the bat started to come around. There was a loud crack, sharp and clear, when the bat connected, and as the ball rose into the air, I felt a real thrill of satisfaction. I was already well on my way to the spot where the ball would come down. I loped easily over, calling for it loudly as I ran. Out of the corner of my eye, I saw Bob Lenney pulling back to let me take it.

Then I turned to plant myself under the ball, reaching up as I did. It was way out in center field, and the grass was deep—and wet. As I turned, I felt my sneakers skid on the wet grass, and before I knew it, I was sitting down. I looked up. I was still under the ball. I forgot about trying to get up. I waited, reached up, and the ball dropped into my glove. I held it up so everybody could see I had caught it.

Then I got up and trotted in.

Mr. Farber was standing by the bat rack when I got there. He was smiling. "Very cool," he said. "Yes sir, just like reaching up to turn off a light. Fine catch, Mickey."

I thanked him and slumped down beside Terry. Terry was grinning. "We're really going to miss you, Mickey," he said. "After a catch like that, we know you're the indispensable center fielder."

"Don't I wish it," I told him. "In this game no one is indispensable."

I was sure, you see, that the team would soon find someone else to gather in those high flies to center. And that really bugged me, because only now was I beginning to have real confidence in my ability. I could feel myself reaching a fine, sharp edge. I felt I knew what I was doing out there, that I would be able to get under anything hit in the air within reason— get under it and catch it. After that bout with my studies, I had gotten kind of rusty; but I was sharp again, really with it, if you know what I mean—only *now* I was off to camp. The thought really curdled me. It was almost as if there were some kind of conspiracy to keep me from playing baseball the way I should.

I sighed and looked out to the plate as Jimmy Kingston stepped up to bat. "Come on, Jimmy!" I yelled. "Sock it over the fence. Then we can all go home."

Jimmy didn't say anything. On the second pitch he swung hard and sent a liner to right field. It was a well-hit ball, and as we jumped up to watch it, we saw that it wasn't going to drop in—but was going to keep right on going over the low, wooden fence in right field.

And that ended the ball game.

After the cheer for the Giants, the team clustered around me. They all knew this was my last game for three weeks.

"Have a good time, Mickey," said Mr. Farber.

49

"We're going to miss you and your famous patented sit-down catch."

"Yeah," said Jimmy Kingston. "They're going to try me back in center, but I'm going to make a determined effort to see if I can catch the ball on my feet."

There was a lot of good-natured banter after that. But I got the message, all right. They really did not want me to go. And to make that point perfectly clear, Mr. Farber overtook me as I started to leave the park with Terry.

"Mickey," he began, "didn't I hear something about your maybe staying here with Terry for the next three weeks instead of going away on the vacation with your family?"

"I tried to sell my father on the idea," I admitted, "but he wouldn't hear of it."

"Oh. That's too bad. Well, have a nice time. And perhaps your father can sneak you back here once in a while to play in a game or two."

"Maybe. But I doubt it."

"Too bad. But three weeks isn't forever, Mickey. And we'll be here when you get back. Nice game."

I thanked Mr. Farber and continued on with Terry in silence. I was thinking hard. In fact, I had been giving this matter some thought these past days and had just about made up my mind what I was going to do. Why not come back here on my own and stay with Terry? Then my father would be able to see just how important baseball was to me.

Who needed a vacation in the mountains anyway?

5

THE LAKE WAS as still as a pane of glass. It was a little after dawn, and patches of mist were still hovering over the water close by the shore. They looked like ghost islands. The sun hadn't hit us yet. And the only sounds were the whippoorwills that were calling in the dark pines along the shore and occasionally the splashing of the fish as they jumped out of the still waters on every side of us.

Audrey was sitting in the center of the canoe, Dad was in the stern, and I was sitting in the bow. All three of us had fishing rods in our hands, and we had been fishing for close to an hour without any luck. We were using night crawlers I had picked up the night before and that I had had to thread onto my hook as well as Audrey's. She absolutely refused to touch what she called "slimy, crawly things." I wouldn't admit it, but I didn't much like poking the hooks through the worms, either.

So far anyway, the worms didn't seem to appeal much to the fish jumping about us in the water. I looked around at the stillness, then sighed and moved to a more comfortable position on my seat. Suddenly Audrey screamed.

I glanced over and saw her pole bending out almost straight while the sound of her unwinding reel filled the air with a high squeal.

"Hang on to it!" Dad cried, reaching over to grab hold of it with her.

But he was too late. The pole had already leaped out of Audrey's hands. I watched it slice into the water and disappear almost at once. In a moment the water was absolutely still again. The fish, the fishing rod, the worm, and the hook were still fleeing somewhere under the quiet waters of Masterson Lake. It had been a brand new fishing rod, too. Audrey began to cry.

Dad reeled in his own line and put down the fishing rod. "It's all right. Don't feel bad. We'll get you a new one."

"You can use mine, Audrey," I said.

She looked at me through her tears. "I'd probably

lose that one, too." She wailed and began to cry even harder.

"Come here, honey," Dad said.

Audrey clambered over a thwart of the boat and settled in Dad's arms, still crying softly. He stroked her head and patted her back, and over her head he winked at me.

"That must have been some whopper of a fish," he said to me. "Hang in there, Mickey. Maybe you'll get one, too."

But I didn't believe him. No such luck, I figured. And besides, all of this really left me cold. I know it sounds crazy to say this now. But, believe me, at the time it really did nothing for me—nothing at all.

After all, the way I looked at it, all this meant for me was that I was almost 150 miles away from Bridgedale—and the Tigers. This was our third day in the mountains. It had taken us this long to get settled in our cabin. The place was isolated. There was not even a phone. And the nearest town—Allens Falls—was on the other side of the lake, across a ridge, and then through a heavy stand of timber—all of it reached by a narrow, rutted, dirt road. I mean this was real wilderness.

But one thing I had noticed. Allens Falls was large enough to have a bus station. I had seen the bus pulling away from a small restaurant as we drove through, and I caught a glimpse of the sign above the windshield. Big, white letters said BRIDGEDALE. That was all I needed to know. I had all my savings with me, and I was sure it would be enough to take me back.

Tomorrow night there was a game with the Indians, and I intended to be out in center field when it started.

Something was grabbing my fishing rod! I grabbed it tightly, looked up, and saw the tip of the rod whipping down toward the water. At the same time, the air was filled with the whining squeal of my reel as the fish fled with the hook in his mouth. I had gotten hold of a big one! With both hands I hung on to the reel.

"Slow down the reel!" my father called.

I did as he suggested, and the tip of the rod disappeared for an instant under the water.

"Reel it in!" Dad called.

I began to tug on the reel, and for a moment I was able to get back quite a bit of line. Then the fish started moving away again, and I had to give it back some of that line. But he soon tired, and again I began reeling him in. This time I got him almost to the canoe before he forced me to pay out more line.

But that was its last gasp.

Dad helped me pull it into the canoe.

"There's our breakfast, Mickey!" he said excitedly. "A beauty! I've never seen a lake trout that big before in my life. Isn't he beautiful?"

The trout was still flopping feebly in the bottom of the boat. I suppose it *was* beautiful, all right. It was long and slender and a sort of olive-grey in color with silver sides that had light spots with soft, red rings around them.

"That's a fifteen-pounder, at least," said Dad. "Wait until you taste him. He'll be delicious pan-fried in butter—and your mother will do it up just fine, if she hasn't forgotten how. Congratulations, Mickey, on catching your first trout."

Audrey was drying her eyes and peering closely at the fish now flopping only once in a while, its gills wide open. "I feel sorry for it," she said. Then she looked at me with a kind of wondering look. "Congratulations, Mickey."

"Sure. Sure," I said. "But you probably would have landed one bigger than this if you could have hung on to your fishing pole."

"Let's get back to the cabin," said Dad, starting to paddle. "Fresh mackinaw trout for breakfast."

Wondering what the trout would taste like, I put

my pole down and started to paddle also. I didn't usually like to eat fish, and Mom seldom cooked it. Now it looked like we were going to get something special. Well, I hoped so.

Later that day—about three in the afternoon—I was sitting by myself on the edge of the dock when I saw Audrey paddling toward me in the little flat-bottom boat that came with the cabin. It was just the right size for her, and she was getting good at handling it. I preferred the canoe though, especially the easy way it sliced through the water. Besides, it was a lot faster. I waved to Audrey and watched her getting closer. I was bored. Dad had driven into Allens Falls to get some provisions. We had done some hiking after breakfast, and after dinner Audrey and Mom had gone to look for blueberries.

Audrey steered for the dock. I got up and reached over and guided her alongside. As she clambered out, I tied up the boat. She was all flushed and excited from her ride.

"Boy," she said, sitting down beside me on the dock. "I can really go in that boat. It's neat!" She looked around. "Where's Dad?"

"Dad's in Allens Falls. He went in to get more supplies."

"Why didn't you go in with him?"

"I didn't feel like it," I said.

She looked at me, her expression disapproving. Then she said, "You're mean."

I looked up at her. "Why? What do you mean?"

"You're not enjoying this vacation at all. I can tell. You just don't want to. Poor Dad. I'll bet he feels awful."

I was surprised. I thought I'd been able to hide the way I felt from Audrey at least. "Think how *I* feel," I said to her. I'd rather be playing ball." I slapped at a mosquito. "I would *much* rather be playing ball than swatting these mosquitoes. And eating lake trout for breakfast."

"Didn't you like it?"

"Sure. It was all right. But not as a steady diet— and it looks like that's the way it's going to be for the next three weeks. Up at the crack of dawn, fishing in the canoe until one of us gets a strike—then in for a fish breakfast."

"Boy," she said, "what an attitude."

"Well, you won't have to put up with it much longer."

"What do you mean, Mickey?"

58

"I'm going back to Bridgedale tonight."

Audrey looked at me for a minute, then tipped her head and smiled. "You're kidding."

"No. I'm not kidding. I'm paddling the canoe over to the other side of the lake tonight. Then I'm walking into Allens Falls and taking the bus to Bridgedale." I took out my wallet and showed her the bulge of bills in the pocket.

She believed me then. "Wow, you *are* serious. Oh, Mickey, you know you shouldn't do that. Please don't."

"It's the only way for Dad to realize that I'm serious about playing ball."

"But you did so well this morning. I mean, look at that great big fish you caught."

I shrugged. "Who needs it? I'd rather play ball."

Dad drove in to camp then. He saw us on the dock and waved to us as he drove past. Both of us waved back to him.

"Don't you tell him," I told Audrey. "If you do, I'll . . ."

She was used to my making all kinds of threats, the way brothers do I suppose, and she acted like she didn't even hear this one. "Please, Mickey. Don't do it. Dad will feel awful."

"You don't understand. I *have* to."

Her voice was soft suddenly. "What time are you going tonight?"

"As soon as Mom and Dad are asleep. They go to bed early up here."

"When is the bus supposed to leave?"

"Remember when we drove through Allens Falls last Saturday night? It was around midnight, wasn't it?"

"I don't know. I was asleep by that time. I don't even remember driving through Allens Falls."

"Well, I remember, and I think I saw a bus just pulling out for Bridgedale. That's the bus I'm going to take."

"How much money do you have?"

"Close to thirty-five dollars."

She whistled softly. "Wow."

I grinned. "I took out all my school savings. I told Mom I might want to buy things on the vacation."

"What are you going to do when you get home?"

"That's easy. I'll stay with Terry—and play ball."

She shook her head. "I wish you wouldn't do it."

"I wish I didn't have to," I admitted.

"Okay, you two!" Mom called to us from the cabin porch. "Let's get in here and get ready for supper."

Audrey and I got up and started for the cabin. All of a sudden I seemed a lot closer to her. I guess it was because I knew she wouldn't tell—even though she didn't want me to do it.

The folks went to bed even before nine o'clock that night and were snoring away long before nine-thirty. My overnight bag had been packed and zippered shut under my bed since suppertime, with my wallet folded in among an extra pair of pants. I didn't want to take any chance of losing that wallet. I grabbed my flashlight and sneaked out through the kitchen. For a while I sat on the back porch to make sure I hadn't wakened anybody, then started for the lake.

"Wait, Mickey!"

I turned. It was Audrey, fully dressed, hurrying through the darkness after me.

"I can help you paddle across the lake," she said.

I thought that over. The lake was a pretty big one and looked even bigger in the darkness. I could use the help. But no—Audrey was too small to paddle this big canoe back across the lake in the middle of the night all by herself.

"You're too small," I said.

"No, I'm not, Mickey. I can paddle back along the shore. I won't go straight across. Please, Mickey. Let me."

"No."

She took a deep breath and looked at me. "If you don't let me go across with you, I'll go right back now and tell Dad what you're doing."

"You wouldn't do that."

"Yes, I would."

But I knew she wouldn't do that. I shrugged. "Go ahead then. Be a rat."

Then I turned my back on her and started for the canoe. We kept it beached in a small cove a little ways down from the dock. But Audrey stuck to me like glue.

"Please, Mickey," she pleaded, "don't go."

I ducked around a pine. "No sense in arguing with me now. It's too late."

"Dad will feel awful. And Mom, too. We'll all miss you, Mickey."

She stopped. "Are you listening to me?"

I smiled at her, although in the darkness I doubted if she noticed. "Sure I am. You said you'd all miss me. I'll miss all of you. But I've *got* to play in tomorrow night's game."

"Oh, Mickey. It's just a *game*. And Dad—he's been looking forward to this vacation with you for months and months. I even heard him talking about it to Mom. He says he's hoping it will bring you and him closer together."

That did make me feel awful. It really did. I suppose I could have turned around and gone back to the cabin right then. But I didn't want Audrey to think she could talk me into anything. And besides this, my mind was made up. At that moment no one could have told me anything.

"No," I said, "you're just saying that. And I know you won't miss me—especially the way I always pick on you."

"Yes, I will miss you, Mickey. It will be lonely up here without you. And Mom and Dad will want to go right home."

"Are you kidding? They're up here now, and they're going to stay. They don't need me to have fun and enjoy themselves. I'll write them as soon as I get home."

That's what I said and that's what I believed, but it was beginning to sound kind of hollow, even to me. Still, I walked to the canoe, dropped my bag into it, and turned to Audrey.

"Go on back now, Audrey," I said.

The moon got brighter suddenly as it sailed out from behind a cloud. I could see Audrey's face clearly. Tears were running down her cheeks.

"Please don't go, Mickey," she said. "I'm scared. You might get lost."

"Now, look! I'm almost thirteen! I can take care of

63

myself! Now, go on. Go back to the cabin. Go on, Audrey. It's getting late." It would have been nice if I had felt at that moment as confident as I sounded.

In a very solemn voice Audrey said, "All right, Mickey."

Right then I wished I could have bent down and hugged her. But she was only my pesky kid sister. I was even surprised at myself for thinking such a thing. I said, "Look, Audrey. You can have my flashlight. You're always wanting to play with it. Here. Take it. Go on. You can have it. But, please, go on back to the cabin now."

She took the flashlight. "Thanks, Mickey! You mean I can really *keep* it?"

"Sure. Now, go on back."

She turned to go, then looked back at me. "Be careful, Mickey."

"Sure. Sure," I said.

She turned and started back toward the cabin. I watched her go for a minute; then splashing into the water, I shoved the canoe's metal keel over the gravel part of the beach until I felt it drop off the shelf of sand into the deeper water. I waded out past the stern and swung into the canoe, then pushed away with the paddle and began paddling straight out. I had a good idea which direction to take. The ridge on the other

64

side loomed visibly against the night sky, and I aimed the canoe at a clump of extra tall pines on top of the ridge.

I paddled hard, and although for a while it looked as if I were not making much progress, I realized soon enough that I was doing just fine. The ridge got gradually larger, the pines taller and more distinct. When I reached the other side of the lake, I found a nice cove and paddled the canoe into it. A line of white sand appeared, and I headed the canoe straight for it.

It didn't take me long to pull the canoe up onto the beach and start into the timber. As I pushed through the woods, I kept my eye on that ridge looming ahead of me against the night sky. It looked like the back of a huge camel. Sometimes the trees around me hid it, and then I wished I hadn't given Audrey my flashlight.

At last I topped the ridge. The moon came out from behind the clouds for a minute, and I saw the dirt road that led to Allens Falls below me like a white ribbon in the forest. As I started down the other side of the ridge, I took one last look at the lake spread out behind me.

I stopped. I thought I had seen a tiny flash of light far out on the lake. I peered at the spot as closely as

I could, but the moon was back behind the clouds, and I couldn't see anything at all except a lot of water. For a moment I thought maybe Audrey might have gotten into that flat-bottom boat and gone after me. But that was crazy. She was a spunky kid, but she wouldn't do anything as foolish as that. Then a couple of fireflies started darting in the air between me and the lake. I realized that this was what I must have seen, so I continued on down the slope toward the road.

I didn't have much trouble finding the restaurant bus stop in Allens Falls where I'd seen the bus pulling out that night. It was still open even though it was close to eleven. I was tired from the walk and was hoping to get something to drink inside the restaurant before the bus came.

I walked in and put my bag down under the lunch counter. "I'd like a glass of milk," I told the woman behind the counter. "A large one."

She didn't say anything, but she stared at me before she turned around and poured out my glass of milk. When she put the glass down before me on the counter, she said, "That will be twenty cents."

I had some change and gave her a quarter. As I

gave it to her, I asked, "Can I get a bus ticket here?"

She rang up the sale and gave me back a nickel. "You say you want to buy a bus ticket?"

I nodded and took a large swallow from my glass of milk.

"Where to?"

"Bridgedale."

"Where's that?"

"Near Phoenix."

"That's a long way from here."

I nodded. "When is the next bus leaving?" I asked.

"For Bridgedale?"

Again I nodded.

"There aren't any. Not any busses leaving for Bridgedale."

"How come?" I said. "I saw one last Saturday leaving for Bridgedale from here."

"You saw the bus going north—to Bridgeport. You didn't read the sign right." She smiled. She was old and tired, and for some reason she seemed to be amused by the fact that I had been mistaken about the sign.

I sagged. This was it. Then I thought of something. "Well, how about a ticket to Phoenix?"

"Sure. There's a bus through here tomorrow afternoon at three. You can take that one if you want."

She was watching me closely, and when she saw the look on my face, she said, "Why don't you go home, kid? Things will look a whole lot better in the morning."

It was as if she had been looking right into my brain and reading all my thoughts. She knew I was running away from something, or at least that's what she thought. Actually, I was running to something— back to my home in Bridgedale where I could do what I wanted.

I finished my milk, picked up my overnight bag, and left the restaurant. I felt frustrated. All of a sudden everything was going wrong. As I stood on the sidewalk trying to decide what to do next, a huge tractor-trailer truck pulled up to the gas pump in front of the restaurant. It was so big I had to step back into the restaurant doorway to let the tractor swing past me. As the driver stepped down and walked toward the restaurant doorway, I cleared my throat.

"Mister?"

He stopped.

"You going far?"

The truck driver looked at me. "How far is far?" He grinned suddenly. "I'm heading for Phoenix. Looking for a ride?"

"Sure."

He studied me for a minute. "How old are you, anyway?"

"Seventeen," I lied. "I'm going back home. I've been visiting a friend."

I waited to see if he believed me. There was not too much light in front of the restaurant, and I have always been tall for my age. Maybe this time it would really be an advantage.

The fellow nodded. "Well, if you're looking for a ride, I'm looking for company. Climb aboard. Soon as I eat something, I'll be on my way."

"Thanks!"

I had trouble opening the cab door. He chuckled, reached up, and wrenched it open for me. "Climb in," he said, "and make yourself at home. There's a sleeping bunk back of the seat if you're tired."

I thanked him and climbed inside. He slammed the door shut behind him, and I lifted my overnight bag onto the bunk and then crawled up after it. The inside of the cab smelled of axle grease and oil. But it was a comforting smell that reminded me of my father's garage back in Bridgedale. I sighed and kicked off my shoes. I was really tired. And then I remembered just how early I had gotten up that morning. That morning. It seemed like a hundred years ago. I closed my eyes. Almost at once I fell asleep.

I awoke with the sound of the truck's motor filling the cab and the beams of oncoming headlights boring into my eyes. I stirred and sat up. The highway's white dividing line was like a long, wiggling tape the truck was swallowing up. For a moment I didn't have any idea where I was. Then I remembered.

"Hi there, kid!" the driver said. "How are the accommodations? Not the most plush, but when you're tired, they do pretty well, hey?"

"Yes, they do," I managed. My throat was dry, and I felt kind of fuzzy. But I remembered the driver telling me if I were looking for a ride, he was looking for company, so I slid down onto the seat beside him.

"How far have we gone?" I asked.

"Allens Falls is a good fifty miles behind us. My name's Abe Sweet. What's yours?"

"Mickey Ortega."

"Going home, eh? Where did you say you live? Phoenix?"

"No. Bridgedale. A few miles south of Phoenix."

"Well, I don't go to Bridgedale. Phoenix is the end

of my haul. But you can get a bus from Phoenix to Bridgedale, all right."

He was right. With all that money in my overnight bag, I'd have no trouble getting a bus to Bridgedale. "Think we might get there by morning?"

"We'll be in Phoenix by morning, Mickey—just in time to see the sun come up—barring any unforeseen accidents such as flat tires and any of the other ills of the American road."

He began to whistle then, after which he started talking. He was a fine, jolly man who was very proud of his family. He had three children—a boy and two girls—and a wife whom he said was the best cook in the world. He talked on and on, and I tried to listen and keep up with him, but soon his voice became part of the motor's roar; and before I knew it, I was asleep again.

When I awoke, the truck was not moving. The driver was gone. I was back up in the bunk, and the large, bright red-and-pink sign of a diner across the highway was pouring its light into the cab. I slid out of the bunk and down onto the seat. Abe was probably in the diner getting his breakfast. I felt thirsty. Abe had parked beside an all-night gas station across the highway from the diner, so I slipped on my shoes, opened the cab door, jumped down, and headed for the gas station. The attendant was sitting behind the cash register reading a book.

"Do you have a cold drink machine?" I asked. He indicated the far side of the station with his thumb and went back to reading. I found the machine in the farthest corner of the station. A small transistor radio was sitting on a shelf, blaring some wild "rock" music. I stood there for a while, about half asleep, enjoying the orange drink and the music, staring at all the things on the shelves—oil cans, flashlights, all sorts of car accessories. It was a mess, but somehow it was fascinating. And it was warm inside the station. I finally finished the drink and stepped outside the building. It was close to dawn, and there was a damp chill in the air. I shivered and started for the truck.

But it was as if I were still asleep—inside a nightmare. Maybe you know the kind I mean. The ones where you go back to find something you left, and it's not there anymore. The truck was gone. With all that music from the radio, I hadn't heard it pull out.

I ran out past the gas pump and looked down the highway. I could see the truck then, pulling through an intersection. I waved frantically and started to run after it, but it kept pulling farther and farther away, growing rapidly smaller in the predawn darkness. I stopped running and looked around.

I was on a busy highway. All around me were stores and diners, and in the distance, outlined against the rapidly brightening sky, were huge smokestacks pumping smoke into the air. I realized I was in the outskirts of Phoenix. Well, all right. No harm done. Now all I had to do was find the bus station and buy myself a ticket for . . .

Then I remembered. My knees turned suddenly to water. My overnight bag with all my clothes and with my wallet containing all that money was still inside the truck!

6

I DIDN'T PANIC. Abe Sweet seemed like an honest man. What must have happened, I figured, was that he had gotten back into the truck and just driven off, thinking I was still asleep in the bunk. He was probably talking all the while, too, probably never even looking back to see if I were still there. I could just see him talking as he put the truck in gear and pulled out of the gas station. That meant he would soon discover that I wasn't in the bunk. And as soon as he found that out, perhaps he would turn around and come back for me.

I didn't panic. I went back to the gas station to wait. The attendant was still inside the station reading. I didn't bother him. I just sat down on the edge of the cement platform next to the gas pumps and waited.

Soon the sun was in my eyes, and I was forced to look away. Then the early morning traffic started, and I had to get away from the pumps as car after car pulled into the station. Then the day attendant arrived. Then the manager. The sun got higher, and the cars piled into the station in a steady stream. Plenty of trucks pulled in also—because of that diner across the highway.

But not the truck driven by Abe Sweet.

About nine-thirty I got a bright idea and left the gas station and went across to the diner. Trucks going the other way were pulling in all the time. I had been watching them for the past half hour. Why not, I had asked myself, find a truck going to Bridgedale? I had had no trouble getting a truck ride from Allens Falls to Phoenix. And it was sure cheaper than a bus. Or it would have been if I hadn't left my wallet in the truck.

I saw a truck driver leaving the diner heading for a big tractor trailer. Before he got to it, I stopped him. "Say, mister, how about a ride? I want to get to Bridgedale."

He was a big, burly guy. I couldn't see his eyes. They were hidden behind dark sunglasses. A toothpick was sticking out of one corner of his mouth. "You a runaway, kid? You don't look old enough to be that foolish."

I didn't want to, but I had to admit it. I nodded sheepishly. "Yes, sir," I said. "I'm a runaway. But I'm trying to get back to my hometown to play ball."

The fellow took the toothpick from his mouth and snapped it and threw it down on the ground. "Sorry, kid. It's against company policy to give anyone a ride. Our insurance doesn't allow it. You might find some gypsy that might give you a ride, but you'd have to be pretty lucky."

Without any further words to me, the fellow moved past me, climbed into his truck, and drove off.

Well, that discouraged me. But I kept asking all the other truck drivers I could find in hopes one of them would take a chance on giving me a ride. But the moment they saw me their faces grew hard, and I could see they were making their minds up to say no before I even asked them for the ride. Some tried to make it easier on me. They said they were sorry and all that, but it was always *no* all the same.

Finally, I gave up. As I left the diner and started to cross the apron in front of it, one of the fellows in the diner came hustling out after me.

"Hey, kid!"

I stopped and turned.

"You won't have any luck hitchhiking around here. There has been a lot of trouble in the last couple of weeks with hitchhikers, so everyone has just about decided not to give anyone a lift. Just thought I'd tell you."

"Thanks," I said.

That was that then. I would have to walk if I wanted to get anywhere, and I had just about decided to go into Phoenix. So I started walking along the highway. The morning chill was gone now—completely. It was hot and getting hotter by the minute. And the panic I had kept down was now slowly overtaking me.

How was I going to get from Phoenix to Bridgedale? Bridgedale was more than forty-five miles away. I didn't have the bus fare, and it didn't look like I would have any luck at all hitchhiking. Oh sure, I could call up Terry and have his father pick me up, but calling Terry's father was definitely not what I wanted to do. I had to go about this business of running away all by myself.

I was just beginning to realize what this trip back to Bridgedale was costing me. I had ended up in the wrong city. I had lost some of my clothes, an overnight bag, and a wallet containing thirty-four dollars. Now I was tired and hungry. I was making a mess of the whole thing, that's what I was doing. And the more I thought about it the more foolish I felt. If I

77

had to end up calling Terry's father—or my father or anyone else for that matter—to come bail me out, I would really look silly. No. I was in trouble, all right. But it was my trouble, and I wasn't going to go running home or call up my friends to come help me.

As I came to this conclusion, my panic faded, and in its place there began to grow a sense of anger—at myself mostly—and determination. I would fight my own way out of this situation. The thought gave me a little courage. I felt better at once and began walking just a little faster, my step a little surer. I almost forgot how hungry I was.

By eleven I reached what I guessed was the main business section of Phoenix. Since I was broke and hungry, I needed some kind of job. My father was always saying that if anyone really wanted work in this country, he could always find something to do if he weren't too proud. Well, I wasn't too proud, not now I wasn't. I went into a restaurant and walked up to the cashier.

"May I speak to the manager, please?"

"The manager?" She smiled, as if I were just too cute or something.

"Yes, the manager," I said, without smiling or looking away.

78

She hesitated for a moment, then said, "Just a moment, please."

She got out from behind the counter and went up to one of the waitresses. She spoke to her quietly, and the waitress turned quickly and looked at me, then nodded to the cashier and went toward the back of the restaurant. The cashier returned to her post and smiled at me. In a friendly way she seemed to want me to tell her what I wanted, but I didn't say anything.

A little man came toward me from the kitchen. He was wearing dark pants and had on a white shirt and bow tie. As he approached me, he was frowning and seemed nervous and uncertain.

"Yes?" he said, glancing quizzically at the cashier, then back at me. "What is it, boy? Have you lost something?"

I almost said 'Yes, my wallet.' "I'd like a job," I told him. "I could wash dishes. Or maybe you could use a busboy."

He smiled then, seeming very much relieved. "Wash dishes? How old are you?"

I swallowed and told him the truth.

He shook his head sadly and put his hand on my shoulder. "You're underage. I couldn't hire you, even if I had an opening. Come back when you're a little older."

That wasn't very much help, but I thanked him and left.

Now what? I'd heard my father talk many times of the time when he was a teen-ager in Dallas and he had washed dishes and sometimes bussed them, whatever that meant. But I was too young. They wouldn't let me. Well, perhaps if I told them I was older, I'd get by. That truck driver seemed to have believed me when I told him I was seventeen.

So I started up again, not as confident as before, but just as determined. About seven or eight restaurants later, I'd lost almost all my confidence and a big part of my determination. Only one manager had even pretended to believe I was sixteen, and he told me to go to City Hall and get my working papers filled out. A real clever way to say no, I thought, and I was right back where I had started from.

It was about one o'clock by that time, and I was really hungry now. Going into the restaurants and standing around waiting to speak to the managers was painful. I could smell all that lovely food, and my mouth would start to water, but I couldn't say anything. Sometimes a tray would go floating by right under my nose, and I just could have reached out and taken some of the food.

Well, I didn't of course, and now there I was standing on the sidewalk, wondering as I watched the people hurrying by me what I was going to do next. They looked like they all had a special place to go, but they didn't seem very happy about it. They looked right through me, as if I were not even there. Still, I envied them. They were going somewhere. And that meant that they were on their way home. Home. I took a deep breath. I guess it was more like a sigh.

Looking back into the restaurant I had just left, I watched the diners at their tables. They looked so content and well fed. And if they ever thought to look out the windows, they were just like the people on the sidewalk. They didn't see me, either. Maybe I should try a different part of town. The restaurants here were all so expensive. It was as if everything—even the people on the street—were behind glass.

But I kept walking until I saw a kid approaching me. Since he looked about my age, I thought he might be able to help. I stopped.

"What are you looking at, kid?" he said, stopping also.

"You," I said.

"Yeah? Well, look someplace else."

I stood my ground. He was about my height but a lot thinner. He had dark eyes and a thin blade of a face that was real dark from the sun. As he spoke, I could see how clear and white his teeth were. His hair was black and hung down over his ears. He looked like an Indian. He had a box or something slung over his shoulder, and his left arm was in a cast from his elbow down. Only his fingers were showing.

"What happened to your arm?" I asked.

He looked at me for a moment without replying. I thought he was trying to decide whether or not he should continue to speak to me. Then he shrugged and said, "I broke it playing stickball." He grinned suddenly. "I slid for home and came down on my arm. You should have heard it snap."

"When did you do it?"

"A week ago."

"Did it hurt?"

"Not then. Later. After they put the cast on."

"Too bad."

"I'll say. I can hardly shine shoes with one hand. It slows me down something awful."

"Is that what you do? Shine shoes?"

"What do you think this shoeshine box is for, looks?"

82

"Is that what it is?"

"You've got to be kidding. You mean you never saw one before?"

"Not where I live."

"Where's that?"

"Bridgedale."

He frowned. "Some small town out in the sticks?"

I nodded. "I guess that's what you could call it."

"Sounds great. You have trees and grass and blue skies, huh?"

"That's right."

"So what are you doing here? You ran away or something?"

"That's too long a story. And right now I'm just hungry."

"You broke?"

I nodded.

Suddenly we saw a fellow getting out of a cab. The man looked rather prosperous from the way he was dressed—red shirt, white tie, and white slacks. The kid moved quickly along beside him.

"How about a shine, mister? Good shine. Special today. Thirty-five cents."

The fellow stopped as if to think it over, looked down at his shoes and then at the kid. "How much?"

"Twenty-five cents."

The fellow grinned suddenly. "That include the tip?"

"Sure."

Then the fellow looked at the kid's wrist. "You got a broken arm there, boy?"

The kid nodded.

"Never mind. Later. See me when you're in better shape. Stay home and take care of yourself."

"I can still shine your shoes, mister. I can do a better job with one hand than most shoeshine boys can do with two."

The fellow frowned, then walked over and leaned back against the building. "Okay," he said. "Show me."

The kid did just that. His right hand fairly flew over the fellow's shoes. He did well until it came to the final buff. His cast gave him some difficulty. The fingers sticking out of the cast couldn't get a very good grip on the buffing cloth. As a result, the buffing suffered somewhat.

"Never mind," the fellow said, flipping the kid a half dollar. "Save your energy. Go home and take a rest or that wrist won't heal right."

The boy watched the man move away, flipping the half-dollar as he watched. Then he looked over at me. "You still hungry? Come on."

84

He took me through a maze of back alleys and down a couple of main streets to a hamburger place on a corner. It was painted a bright orange and white, and the hamburgers sizzling on the grill smelled as good as they sounded. We slid up on plastic stools. The kid put his box down beside him on the counter.

"Two burgers," he said.

I watched hungrily as the short-order cook slid a spatula under a well-done patty, slapped it down onto a roll, and in one swift motion laid it on a plate and passed it to me. I reached for it eagerly, but before my aching jaws could close over the hamburger, the kid pulled it away from me and reached over for the mustard and relish.

"Load up on the relish," he said softly. "Really load up. That stuff's free—and it's filling."

I followed his advice, and when I finally got to eat my hamburger, I could barely taste it along with all the mustard and relish. But it *was* filling and almost a meal in itself.

"What do you want to drink?" the kid asked me.

"That orange soda," I said, indicating a bubbly glass tank.

He nodded and ordered a glass of milk for himself and the orange drink for me. When we had finished, we left the place. Once outside I stuck out my hand.

"Thanks," I said. "My name is Mickey Ortega."

"You're welcome, kid. My name is Charlie Johnson. My father's a full-blooded Cherokee, if you didn't notice."

"I noticed."

"You're a Mexican-American, huh?"

"That's right."

"Do you want to tell me what you're doing in Phoenix?"

I told him. It took awhile, and when I was finished, he just shook his head. "I won't say anything. I'd just make you mad, and you wouldn't learn anything."

"Thanks," I said, grinning ruefully.

"Well now. You're going to need a job, all right—that is if you insist on not calling up your folks or someone you know in Bridgedale."

"There's no phone at the camp," I said. "And I'm not going to ask my friend Terry's father to drive all the way to Phoenix for me. No. I can take care of myself. That's what I kept telling my sister, and I'd better prove I can, or she'll never let me hear the end of it."

"Well, you're too young to get a job in a restaurant like you said you had tried."

"I've got an idea."

"Go on."

"You don't do so well with one hand. Let me polish shoes for you, and we'll split fifty-fifty."

He thought that over for a minute, then said, "I've got a better idea. I know where we can get another shoe box. You could be my partner. And you can do the buffing for both of us. We split fifty-fifty whatever we get. It's a good deal, because I'll be teaching you the business, and you'll be earning while you're learning." He grinned. "Sounds just like TV, huh?"

"Okay," I said. "Sounds great."

"Come on, then. We need to see the fellow who has the extra shoeshine box."

It turned out that we had to pay for the shoeshine box. The kid wanted six dollars for it, and when I saw the flat he lived in, I could understand why he needed the money. But Charlie talked him into lending it to me until I could earn the money to pay for it. It ended up that I had three days to come up with the six dollars, or the kid could take it back.

Then about three that afternoon my apprenticeship began as I learned how to polish a shoe—any shoe, no matter how scuffed—to a high sheen. First thing, I had to clean off all the dirt with a stiff brush. Then I put on a coat of shoe polish, brushed it to a high polish, then added still another coat and polished that. Then came the buffing with the cloth. Charlie had trouble showing me that, especially the snap. But he was able to get me to do it finally, and by the time I finished my first lesson, his shoes were beautifully polished, if I do say so myself.

Then I put in my own two-cents. I convinced Charlie to leave this section of town and go to the broad avenues where I had first tried to get a job. The people I had seen walking along those streets looked like they thought polished shoes were important enough to pay well to have them done. When Charlie protested that those people seldom if ever tipped, I convinced him that together we would make up in volume what we lost in tips.

Business was good, right from the start. Charlie would spot a likely prospect—someone who looked nervous about his appearance usually—and would fall in step beside him and say something like this: "Nice pair of shoes there, mister. How about a shine to keep them nice? My partner and I are fast—and inexpensive. Thirty-five cents. That's all. A quality pair of shoes like that deserves the best."

And he smiled all the while he talked, his white

teeth flashing in his dark face. By the time he finished his spiel, he would be near the place where I was standing against the building, and four out of ten times, the man he was talking to would shrug and veer over toward me. Then Charlie would go after another customer. And when we both were polishing shoes side by side, he would give me hints on how to use the brush more effectively and watch to make sure I didn't miss any spots.

We quit around seven o'clock, each of us a couple of dollars and a little change richer. I realized I would have my shoeshine box paid for before long. But I would still be a long way from getting the bus fare I needed to get to Bridgedale. And as Charlie and I entered the usual hamburger place for our supper, I couldn't help noticing how the streets were emptying of people as they went home.

Home. Again I was thinking of home. Everyone had one to go to, I realized as I looked out of the window and started to eat my hamburger. Everyone, that is, except me. I wondered if Charlie had a home.

But I was a big boy now. I was almost thirteen, so I didn't need a home or a family. And here I was in Phoenix learning how to polish shoes. I saw a little girl running down the sidewalk to her mother, her arms outstretched, and right away I thought of Audrey. She hadn't wanted me to make this trip—and oh, how right she had been.

I almost choked on the hamburger, and as I tried to swallow it down, Charlie nudged me. "Come on, Mickey. We don't want to miss the theater crowd. And the theaters are about ten blocks from here."

"Okay. Okay," I managed. "Just let me finish this, will you."

"Sure, partner. Sure."

I looked away from the window and tried to decide what I would have to drink. When I saw Charlie drinking his milk, I decided that I would order some, too, even if it made us a little late. Milk was good for you, and it was about time I started doing what was good for me.

7

WE DIDN'T DO spectacularly with the movie and theater crowd, just a couple of shines each. After we finished around nine o'clock, I thought we could call it a day. I was bothered about where I would sleep that night. I had seen some places that advertised rooms for the night, but I didn't much like the looks of them. Besides, if I gave them the three dollars they wanted, that would cut into what I had put away for the shoeshine box.

But instead of quitting, Charlie led me to a large old hotel behind the movie district. Together we sneaked into the side entrance. From there we went down into the lower lobby.

"They let me polish shoes here," he said. "The man who used to be in the main lounge quit two years ago, and I know the head bellhop. He's from my street."

"Good," I said. "But how long are we going to stay in this hotel?"

"All night. A friend of my family, the bellhop—Arnie's his name—lets me sleep in the top floor linen room. He won't mind if you do, too." Then he thought of something. "Around ten-thirty we've got to leave here, though, and make the rounds of the movie houses."

"What for?"

Just then a fellow came into the lower lobby.

"Shine, mister?" Charlie asked him.

The fellow looked down at his shoes, then at Charlie. "Okay. Make it snappy."

As Charlie set to work unpacking his shoe box and lining up his polish and brushes on the carpet, he looked up at me and answered my question. "We put up the seats for the cleaning crew. Any wallets we find get turned in. That's part of the deal."

He began to polish the man's shoes. When he got to the buffing, I took over, snapping the cloth like a real professional.

The fellow tossed me a half-dollar. I dug in my pocket for a quarter and handed it to Charlie.

"Thanks, partner," he said.

We walked over and sat down on one of the

couches along the wall. It felt so good to relax on something soft. I looked around. The lobby was very large. The dark, faded maroon carpet was deep and soft to walk on. On all the walls large pictures—mostly of beautiful countrysides with lots of clouds in the skies—were hung inside old-looking frames.

"This is a pretty nice place," I said.

"It used to be the finest hotel in Phoenix. But that was a long time ago, according to Arnie. When they moved the train station, it lost most of its business. It's kind of seedy now, Arnie says—but I like it. Sometimes, if the cleaning woman sees me and it's late enough, she leaves a door to one of the suites on the top floor open for me, and I get to sleep in a big bed all by myself with clean, cool sheets—so clean you can just smell how fresh they are. Know what I mean?"

I nodded. Yes, I knew just what he meant. Mom changed the sheets on Saturday, and after I'd taken my bath, I would climb into bed and pull the fresh sheets over me. It felt great. On those nights, it seemed, I always slept just a little more soundly than usual.

My thoughts went racing back to home then, and from home to the camp. As it did I felt a sudden clutch of dismay. This was all so crazy—unreal—

93

that I should be here in this big old hotel in Phoenix. Just the day before I had been in camp with my folks. Was it only a day ago? It was difficult to accept all that had happened to me in one short day. I thought again of the camp and imagined that I could hear the echoing calls of the birds coming from the other side of the lake and the whippoorwills we had heard in the boat that morning when I caught the fish. As I pictured it all to myself, I almost fell asleep. I shook myself awake, then leaned back again. This time I did fall asleep.

Charlie was shaking me. "Mickey. It's time to go. We've got to hit the theaters now."

I groaned. "Now? What time is it?"

"It's almost ten. Come on!"

I didn't want to go. I was so tired. And the soles of my feet suddenly seemed tender and swollen from all the walking I had done that day on the miles and miles of cement sidewalks.

But I roused myself and followed after Charlie, stumbling along as if I were walking in my sleep. I didn't get fully awake until we hit the first movie theater, the Rialto I guess it was, and went inside. The head usher was waiting for Charlie and nodded to him to go on in. As we did, he passed Charlie a flashlight. Another usher gave me his, and the two of us started slapping up the seats, two aisles at a time.

Slamming up seats is not exactly the most exciting job in the world. And after the first couple of hundred seats, you really get tired. But you keep moving, stepping over the remains of popcorn, chocolate bars, half-empty cups of soft drinks, and chewing gum. I didn't envy the clean-up crew coming in the next morning with with their push brooms. We worked a total of six movie houses in all.

It was twelve o'clock when we finished our last theater and headed back to the hotel. As we passed one of those outside telephone booths, Charlie stopped to make a call. I waited outside on the sidewalk for him to finish. He was whistling when he stepped out.

"Who did you call?"

"My mother. I always try to check in about this time."

That certainly surprised me. Up until this time, he hadn't said a word about his mother, although he had once mentioned his 'family.' I had wondered if Charlie had a home, but if he were sleeping in a hotel and eating out all the time, I figured he probably didn't have one. "Where does your mother live?" I asked.

"She lives on Water Street. We have a small house, just barely enough room for all of us. I have two brothers and two sisters. I'm the oldest, so I sleep out whenever I'm far from home on my shoeshine and theater jobs."

I nodded. I thought it would be more polite not to ask any more questions, but I was curious, especially since he hadn't mentioned anything about a father. What could have happened to him, I wondered.

As we continued on our way back to the hotel, without my prodding or asking any questions, Charlie began to talk about his mother, his two brothers, and two sisters. Pretty soon I had the whole picture. Charlie's father had just left the Army and was finishing up his education at a school in Oklahoma City. He was learning how to be a civil engineer —something like that. Mrs. Johnson and the children remained in Phoenix, as they owned the little house on Water Street, and by living there, the family could make the G.I payments stretch farther. Charlie's mother let Charlie work as a shoeshine boy in the summer to help with the finances until his father finished school.

"After all," he said, turning a corner, "I'm almost

thirteen, so until Dad gets out of this school, I'm really the head of the family—as far as my brothers and sisters are concerned. That's what Mom says. Anyway, I won't always be shining shoes. Dad'll be back by the end of summer, and I'm doing fairly well at school. When I graduate from high school, I hope I get a scholarship to the Phoenix Business School and study to become a certified public accountant." His teeth flashed in his dark, narrow face. "I really like math, and it's a good-paying profession."

He seemed certain that that was what he was going to be, just as I felt about becoming a ballplayer. But somehow I felt a little uneasy about comparing my ambition to become a Major League ballplayer with his ambition to become an accountant.

Charlie looked down at his broken wrist. "One thing I've got to remember, though, from now on: no more stickball, or baseball or other games like that for a while. I could have really hurt myself, and *then* where would Mom have been? Even as it is, I think maybe this cast has cut down on my tips. The customer can't really believe I can give him a good shine with one of my hands in a cast—and he's right. I can't, really. It's the buffing that brings the tip—that high sheen you get. It convinces them it was a good idea to stop and get the shine and makes them walk

97

off stepping a little more smartly. Know what I mean?"

I nodded. What he said made good sense, but we were back to the hotel by this time, and the sight of it made me suddenly exhausted.

I don't think I had ever been so tired in my life. I remember only dimly Charlie's leading me past the darkened newsstand into the side lobby and over to the elevators. I remember the sudden lift of the elevator's floor, and then its quick dip as we reached the twelfth floor. And then the linen room. Charlie pulled down a lot of sheets and laid them out on the floor like a mattress. I kneeled down on them and then stretched out. I must have been asleep before I finished stretching out.

Someone was shaking me—hard. With some difficulty I opened my eyes. It was Charlie.

"Hey, Mickey!" he urged. "Get up. It's late, close to ten o'clock. Boy, you really are a deep sleeper."

I rubbed my eyes and sat up, then looked around and began to remember where I was. Charlie was holding a white paper bag. "What have you got in there?"

"Your breakfast. I already had mine, so I brought

yours back. I just couldn't get you up before. But we've *got* to move now. We have to put the linen back and get out of this closet before the day help gets up to this floor."

I nodded groggily, got up, and helped him put things back. The sheets we had slept on and which were now a little wrinkled, he carefully folded and placed on the very bottom of the pile on the shelf. "They never get to these sheets," he explained. "This hotel never gets that many guests anymore."

We went down the back stairs and out the service entrance, the trip down the stairway for twelve floors a very long and dizzying one. Once we reached the sidewalk, my aching stomach could hold off no longer, and I plunged my hand into the bag and hauled out a hamburger. It tasted good, even if it was cold.

And then we went to work. We had a good morning. By one o'clock we had made almost six dollars between us—and I was getting a lot of tips. So for lunch I had *two* hamburgers and *two* glasses of milk.

Watching me, Charlie shook his head. "You'll get sleepy eating that much."

I didn't say a word. I just continued devouring my second hamburger.

Charlie was right, of course. I did feel sleepy during the first part of the afternoon, and I didn't get as many tips. But I was fast becoming a good shoeshine boy, and I was proud of my speed as well as the shine I could give. It got so I even looked forward to shining badly scuffed shoes—the ones that offered me a real challenge.

By six o'clock we had cleared nearly four more dollars to give me a total of five dollars for the day. I stopped into a cigar store and exchanged most of my change for crisp one dollar bills and left the place, counting them over and over. With what I had made the day before, I now had more than enough to pay for my shoeshine box. At this rate, I should have enough for my bus fare to Bridgedale.

But when I thought of going to Bridgedale, my enthusiasm faded. My folks were at the camp—and that, suddenly, was where I wanted to go. But earning that much money would really take a long time unless I called my folks and asked them to send me the bus fare. No, I could not do that! I had already settled that with myself. I would work with Charlie for another week or so and then take the bus back to the camp.

And then it occurred to me. Wouldn't I first have to let my folks know where I was and what I was doing?

It's funny how suddenly that thought came to me and the time when it did. I should have thought of that the first thing when I woke up that morning. By yesterday morning Audrey would have told Mom and Dad I had gone back to Bridgedale; but what if my father had called Terry's father to ask about me —to see if I had made it safely?

The moment I asked myself the question I knew what the answer was. Like a lightning bolt or something hitting me out of the blue, I knew at once that he *must* have called, that he *did* call, and that right at that minute he and Mom were asking themselves where I was and what had happened to me.

Charlie and I were heading for our favorite hamburger place when all this occurred to me, and we were just about to cross a street when I pulled up. Charlie looked at me.

"What's the matter, Mickey?"

"I've got to get to a phone."

"All of a sudden? What's the rush?"

So I told him, as quickly as I could, and he fished into his pocket for some change. Then he pointed to a phone booth down the block.

"We can call from there."

I hurried toward it. Once I reached the booth and stepped inside, I had a little difficulty in knowing whom to call first. My mind was racing like a runaway motor. Charlie must have seen how nervous I was, because he stepped into the booth with me.

"Here," he said, "let me."

He dropped the coin into the slot and picked up the receiver. "Now who do you want to call first?"

"My folks."

"Okay. What's their number?"

"They don't have a phone. Not at the camp, they don't."

"Then how are we going to call them?"

"Maybe we could call someone at Allens Falls, and they could get in touch with my folks."

"Okay. Who do we call at Allens Falls?"

"I don't know."

Charlie hung up the receiver. The dime clicked down to the return slot, and he fished it out. "Unless we know who we're calling, Mickey, we can't make the call."

"How about the Post Office?"

"Okay. We can try it. What's the number?"

"I don't know."

"That's all right. We can get it from information."

He put the dime back in and dialed information. The operator was very helpful, and he got the number. She even told him how much it would cost to call that far. Fifty-five cents.

102

So I dropped in two quarters and a nickel after the operator rang the Post Office in Allens Falls. At last someone answered, and Charlie handed me the receiver.

"Yes?" I heard. It sounded like the person was talking from the other end of a long tunnel. It was a woman's voice.

"Would you please tell me if you could deliver a message to my folks?" I asked her. "They have one of those cabins out on the lake."

She said she couldn't hear me and asked me again what I wanted. When I told her, half-shouting it into the phone, she said she thought I should talk to the postmaster. There was a long delay. When she came back to the phone, she sounded a little angry and said the postmaster was out, the Post Office was closed, and that I should call back the next day. Then she added that they didn't deliver parcels to the summer people out on the lake. They usually came into town for them. The operator broke in then to tell me my time was up, and I hung up.

How could I get in touch with my folks?

And then I thought of Terry. If my father had called his house, he might have left a phone number where I could get in touch with him when I did show up in Bridgedale.

This time I put the dime into the slot myself, got

103

the long distance operator, and gave her Terry's number in Bridgedale. In a moment I could hear the phone ringing on the other end. It rang and rang. I kept the receiver glued to my ear until at last the operator broke in to tell me that there was no answer and that perhaps I should place my call later.

Then I remembered. It was close to six-thirty by this time. Tonight was the game with the Yankees. It was an important game. The whole family had probably gone to watch Terry play. And it wouldn't be over until eight-thirty, at least.

I hung up and told Charlie why I hadn't gotten any answer.

He looked at me and gave his head a shake. "Boy, you guys really take your Little League ball seriously, don't you?"

I nodded. "I guess we do. But don't you like to play ball?"

"Sure," he said, holding up his cast. "You bet I do. And look what it cost *me*. But maybe stickball isn't as much fun as Little League ball. We sure don't bother with uniforms or umpires. We just grab a stick and get hold of a tennis ball or a rubber ball and start playing in the street outside our house. Hey, that reminds me. You can't call anyone now, so come on home with me. I want to give my mother what I have made so far."

"Let's eat first," I said.

"Good idea," he said, heading for a hamburger place on the next corner.

I didn't say anything, but I was beginning to get pretty tired of those hamburgers. With no enthusiasm at all, I followed Charlie down the street.

Charlie's mother opened the door just a crack when he knocked. In the dim light of the hallway, I could see how dark her long hair was and how large and beautiful were her eyes. As soon as she saw who it was, she smiled and opened the door all the way. At once little kids sort of exploded into view, jumping up and down in excitement as Charlie entered the house and closed the door.

Then they saw me. At once they quieted. Charlie's mother smiled at me, however, and right away I felt at home.

"This is Mickey, Mom," Charlie said. "He's my new partner."

"Hello, Mrs. Johnson," I said. "Pleased to meet you."

At that, the rest of the family returned to the attack, you might say. The three smallest ones stole slowly toward me, while the oldest one—a little girl —hurried right up to Charlie and began hugging him.

Charlie ignored them as he went into the kitchen, took the change and the bills out of his pocket, and emptied it out onto the table. Right away he gave the little girl hanging on to him a dime, then distributed a nickle each to the three other children. It was easy to see then why his entrance had caused such excitement.

We sat down at the table while his mother stood and counted the money. Counting what he had made the day before, it added up to eight dollars and some change. She pushed a dollar back to Charlie, then leaned over and kissed him on the forehead. "Thanks, Charlie," she said. "How's the wrist?"

"Fine. Just fine. It's beginning to itch a little under the cast."

"That means it's getting better," she said hopefully. Then she looked at me. "So you're Charlie's partner. He told me about you on the telephone last night. Don't you have a home?" She seemed as if she were really concerned about me.

"Sure, I do," I said. "As soon as I get enough money, I'm taking a bus back."

"Did you run away, Mickey?"

I nodded and started to say something.

But she put up her hand and smiled. "No need to explain." She turned to Charlie and me. "I have some chocolate cake. How about a piece and a glass of milk?"

We both liked that idea. The cake was delicious, and we were soon finished.

"We have to go," Charlie said. "Business calls. Right, partner?"

"Right," I answered, and thanked Mrs. Johnson for the cake and milk as I got up and followed Charlie out of the kitchen.

Looking over my head at Charlie, she said, "You take care of Mickey, Charlie. See to it that he gets that bus fare and gets home. Hear?"

Charlie grinned. "Don't worry, Mom."

Once in the street Charlie said, "Okay, partner, we have a job to do—get you home!"

He was right. I wanted to call Terry's house so badly, I began to sweat. But it was only seven-thirty. The game couldn't possibly be over by this time.

So we went back to the theater section to work. We did a little better this evening, but then as the crowd thinned, we headed back to the hotel. Charlie went in by the side lobby past the newsstand. He decided to buy a candy bar. I waited impatiently for him to finish making his selection, since I was anxious to call

107

Terry. Then I happened to glance down at the newspapers. There were quite a few of them. The headlines were mostly about an earthquake in Chile, but one of them had a story about two kids lost in the mountains near Allens Falls.

I looked closer and read:

> ALLENS FALLS, N.M. Troopers have called in a team of bloodhounds to comb the area around Masterson Lake as the search for Mickey and Audrey Ortega, the brother and sister missing since Tuesday, continued into its second day. Their canoe and flat-bottom boat were found floating in the lake Tuesday. Dragging operations started soon after a team of skindivers was flown in from Bridgeport 80 miles north . . .

I couldn't read anymore. I just stared at it and then looked away. Charlie saw my face. "What is it now, Mickey?"

"My sister," I managed. "Audrey. She followed me across the lake and never made it back to the cabin!"

And then I couldn't say anymore. I didn't *dare* say anymore. What I was thinking was just too terrible.

8

CHARLIE GOT IT all out of me eventually, even though I guess I wasn't very easy to understand. I just couldn't keep inside me what I felt—and I felt pretty sick. It was all my fault—*my* fault. I broke down and began to cry.

It was Charlie who pulled me out of it. We went out of the hotel and around into the alley in back. Once there, he shook me hard, his heavy cast digging cruelly into my shoulder.

"Acting like this isn't going to get you anywhere!" he said. "And it isn't going to help your sister, either. They haven't found her yet, so she's probably alive out in the woods somewhere. You ought to go help find her since you were the last one to see her."

I stopped crying and looked at Charlie. He was

right. Maybe Audrey hadn't drowned. But how could I get back? How? I'd already decided against hitch-hiking. Maybe, just maybe, I might find another truck driver like the first one. But no, I had already tried that.

And then I knew there was only one way for me to get back to Allens Falls. I would simply have to go to the police.

"The police," I said, looking straight at Charlie. "Let's find a policeman."

Charlie nodded his head in agreement, and we left the alley.

I couldn't find a policeman anywhere. Then I saw a patrol car cruising slowly by. I waved to the police-man driving, but he didn't see me. I ran out between two parked cars and waved a second time. This time he saw me and slammed on the brakes.

"What is it, kid?" he asked, leaning his head out the window.

I started to tell him all in a rush, and he held his hand up and smiled. "Hold it, kid. Start from the beginning."

"I'm Mickey Ortega. They're looking for me and my sister. They think we drowned or got lost in the woods around Allens Falls, but we didn't. I mean, *I'm* here in Phoenix."

The policeman sitting beside him on the front seat leaned over and said, "Hey, Mike, he's talking about that hunt up north for those two kids."

The first policeman looked quickly back at me. "Get in, kid. We'll take a ride to the station and straighten this out."

I hesitated for just a moment.

"Come on, kid," said the other policeman. "We won't bite you. And if what you say is true, we'll get you back where you belong, pronto."

That did it. I nodded to Charlie, pulled the door open, and climbed in, Charlie right behind me.

Things moved pretty fast after that. They called the sheriff in Allens Falls and got my description from him. That confirmed my story, and the next thing I knew I was on my way to the Phoenix airport. Once there, I said a hasty good-bye to Charlie, gave him the money I had made and the shoeshine box, and climbed into a helicopter.

Any other time I would have enjoyed the ride. We flew through the night low and fast, the tops of trees and houses becoming indistinct blobs as I looked through the plastic bubble. But like I said, this was not the time for me to enjoy such a ride. I was thinking of Audrey—and my folks.

As we dropped down toward the airstrip outside Allens Falls, I saw them standing beside a trooper's car, caught in a circle of light. The moment the helicopter came to rest, I jumped down and raced across the grass toward them. I flung myself into Mom's arms and hung on. As I did, I felt Dad's hand resting on my head, mussing my hair gently. And then I was hugging him, too.

On the ride back to the search area in the patrol car, I told them what I had been doing the last couple of days. They listened without scolding, just nodding every now and then—and I knew they were trying to understand what had come over me to make me take off like that to Phoenix. At the same time, they were trying to keep their anxiety for Audrey from breaking out.

Imagine how I felt when I moved into the circle of lights around a campfire the main body of searchers had built and explained to the trooper in charge of the search what had happened. I told him about that light I had seen on the water when I had looked back. By now I had just about convinced myself that I had really seen a light. It could have been Audrey using my flashlight to help see across the dark water.

As I explained all this, I could hear murmurs and even some muttering as a few of the searchers about me began to realize that this whole incident had been caused by a kid who just wanted to play Little League baseball.

By the time I finished telling my story, I was really tired. My folks led me to a tent and a bunk. I fell asleep almost as soon as I pulled the scratchy army blanket around me. But even as I dropped off, I thought of Audrey—and felt a pang of fear.

The next day, bright and early, I took the trooper in charge—a Captain Trent—to the spot on the ridge where I had seen the light. He nodded and led a tall, gangling fellow with a pack of hounds to the lake-shore in that direction. There was a lot of lake front-age to cover, and it took most of the morning before we came to a spot along the shore that had small islands and sandbars. If Audrey had come ashore there, it would have been a bad spot. Still, if I had been right about the direction that light had seemed to come from, she must have come ashore somewhere around here. We started spashing out onto the shallow, reed-covered islands and soon found all the evidence we needed that Audrey had landed her flat-bottom boat here. For one thing, with Audrey's sweater to remind them, the bloodhounds found her scent and began pulling their trainer through the swampy, marshy land.

Someone found a trace of the boat where Audrey had beached it on a sandbar. But it was just a trace. She obviously hadn't beached it very well. We could see her footprints heading toward the land. As I looked at them, I could imagine Audrey jumping out of the boat and—feeling her feet sink into the soft ground—pulling frantically for the shore. At times her footprints disappeared entirely. But in places where the ground was more solid we could clearly see her small footprints. In the darkness she must have been confused. Her tracks went this way and that, which was the reason the bloodhounds seemed to be going in every direction at once.

We spread wide to find all the tracks we could. It was Trooper Trent who pointed out that there was no sign that Audrey had made it back to the boat. In fact, he reminded us there was every evidence to indicate that Audrey would not have dared try to go back out over this marshy land once she had made it safely to shore. Once we reached solid ground, they let the hounds go. They went off along the lakeshore to the spot where I had beached my canoe. And there we found Audrey's tracks, undisturbed, plain as day, showing where she walked right up to my canoe. There also was the mark the canoe had made in the sand.

"Well, here's where she must have gotten into the canoe," said someone.

"Where she *tried* to get in, you mean," Trooper Trent said. "She must have given up on the flat-bottom boat. Maybe it was morning by this time. She was unable to find Mickey and perhaps—if the boat had floated away—she might have seen it and realized the only way she could get back over the water was to try to paddle this canoe back." Trooper Trent looked at me. "Does that sound like Audrey, Mickey? I mean, would she think herself able to paddle this canoe back?"

I nodded. "Yes, she even wanted to help me paddle across the lake, but I wouldn't let her. I told her she was too little."

Trooper Trent looked grim. "And, of course, she wouldn't believe that." He looked down at the canoe and then around him at the shore. "Look!"

We followed his pointing finger and saw Audrey's tracks leaving the water about ten feet farther down the shore.

"All she managed to do," said the trooper, "was push the canoe into the water. Getting into it was something else again." He looked at me. "Thanks, Mickey. We found the canoe and the flat-bottom boat near the north shore of the lake. That's why we concentrated our search along that shore. Here along the south shore is where we should have been looking." He turned to the others then. "Let's go!"

But we soon lost Audrey's trail in the thick, marshy shoreline. She seemed to be trying to follow it back to the cabin. Around six o'clock that day, I was pretty discouraged, along with everybody else. And Mom and Dad looked terrible. Mom's eyes were red, the flesh under them puffy. She looked scared and kind of desperate. Like Dad. I'd never seen his face so white or his eyes so filled with pain. As they built a fire for supper, I went off by myself and sat on a rock and looked out over the lake.

A twig snapped behind me. I turned to see my father approaching.

"I'm sorry, Dad."

He sat down beside me on the boulder. "I know, Mickey. I know."

116

"Audrey's tough," I said. "She'll be all right."

"Of course." He looked at me. "This boy you met in Phoenix, Mickey. He sounds like quite a resourceful young man, shining shoes to help his mother."

"Yes, Dad."

"Did you mind shining shoes, Mickey?"

I shook my head. "I needed the money, and I didn't want to go crying to you for it."

He placed his hand on my shoulder. "I guess I understand that."

That hurt. He was being so nice, both he and Mom. And all the while Audrey was out there somewhere, lost, maybe crying now as night started to fall.

After supper we turned inland and started a slow sweep back the way we had come—but a lot farther inland this time. The ground was more solid now—and suddenly the dogs caught Audrey's scent and flew off through the thickest portion of the woods.

By this time it was pretty dark. It was difficult for us to see where we were going. And the poor fellow hanging onto the dogs was having a time. But only when they lost Audrey's scent in a marshy area did we pull up to make a camp for the night.

Other searchers were arriving to join us. There was

a great deal of excitement in the air. We all had a feeling we were on the right track and we'd soon find Audrey. Dad looked a lot better. He even smiled now and then. And Mom, too. Her voice didn't sound quite so edgy.

But we still had to wait until daybreak. And I kept thinking of Audrey out on this cold night, probably huddled under some tree, hungry, maybe scratched from briars and thorns. But we did have to wait. And maybe early in the morning we would find her. Maybe.

I walked slowly away from the campfire, keeping it in view as I climbed a ridge. I didn't tell my father. I didn't want him to worry. But I promised myself I would keep the campfire in sight and not get lost. I just couldn't sit still now around the warm fire, and I was too excited to sleep. At last I reached the top of the ridge and looked out over the sea of treetops. There were so many trees it was a real wilderness. The direction Audrey was taking would lead her deeper and deeper into that forest I saw stretching almost endlessly out in front of me.

In my mind's eye, I could just see her struggling through the deep woods, maybe even crying a little, trying to get back to the camp.

And then finding she was lost.

118

I thought I saw something. I stood up. I couldn't be sure, but it looked for a moment like a pale ghost of a light shining at me through a clump of trees far below. I stared at the spot, my heart pounding in my throat, waiting for the light again. It was so far away. Maybe it was just my imagination.

I saw it again, a pale, yellow light glowing for just an instant far down among the trees.

I turned and yelled back to my father. "Dad! Come here! I think I see something."

The noise of the searchers ceased. I heard my father's voice calling to me.

"Where are you, Son?"

"I'm up here, Dad. Up here!"

I started to wave my arm. I guess someone saw it against the night sky, and I heard people start rushing through the brush toward me. I looked back at where I had seen the light. I didn't dare take my eyes off the spot. When they reached me, I pointed to it.

"There! Over there! I saw something. I think it's Audrey with my flashlight. The light was dim. The batteries are probably running low."

"I don't see anything, Mickey," the trooper said.

"Just keep looking," my father said in a hoarse voice. "Keep looking."

The whole crowd of us stood there on that ridge

119

peering down into that dark forest, waiting. And when the light came again, we all saw it at the same time.

There was no doubt this time. Someone was down there moving through the trees, and whoever it was had a flashlight.

"Go back and get some torches from the campfire," said the trooper. "Everybody. We're going down there tonight."

I'll never forget that rush through the darkness, down the ridge and across a swampy area, our torches held high, our feet heavy with mud. We were whipped by the branches, and we stumbled I don't know how many times, but we didn't seem to mind. We kept going, fanning out into a long line, shouting encouragement to each other, the dark woods jumping wildly from the light of our torches.

But it was a long way. From the top of that ridge it hadn't seemed so long, but that was because you couldn't see the swampy patches, the ridges, and the thick underbrush. Soon my side was beginning to ache from the exertion. Gradually, a few began to hang back until finally the trooper called for a halt so that we could regroup and catch our breath.

I could see it was a good idea halting when we did. But despite the pain in my side, I didn't want to stop. I edged away from the searchers and peered ahead through the trees. I had my torch, so I wasn't afraid of getting lost, and I could hear the trooper talking to the rest of the searchers clearly as I moved deeper into the woods ahead of the rest of them. I didn't run. I walked swiftly, my elbow in front of my face to ward off the branches. I topped a rise, my torch held high, and peered ahead, hoping for some sign of Audrey.

At that moment, something rushed at me out of the darkness and flung itself into my arms like something wild. The flashlight clattered to the ground beside me. I dropped my torch and hugged Audrey.

She had found *me*.

9

THAT TROOPER HAD been right. As Audrey told me later, she never did get the flat-bottom boat beached properly in the darkness and lost it right away. Later, when she found the canoe, all she could do was rock it to get it off the beach. But that didn't do any good, so then she had to push it, and when she finally did get it free, it slipped away from her too quickly into the deeper water. She was afraid she would get the flashlight I had given her wet if she started to swim after the canoe. Even worse, she might drop it and lose it in the water, so she went back to shore and started walking.

Following the lakeshore was too difficult for her. Then she decided she didn't need to follow it, since she had the flashlight. That was how she got lost. She was trying to follow a stream back to the lake when we found her. Twice before she had tried, only the stream always got lost in a marsh or a swamp. She was frightened to death of quicksand, so each time she had turned back.

Well, I don't need to tell you what a mess all this made of my father's vacation. As soon as Audrey had rested and had eaten something, we started back to Bridgedale. Funny. I had wanted to get back to Bridgedale so badly so I could play ball, and yet, the closer we got to Bridgedale on the long drive back, the worse I felt.

I didn't even feel much better when I learned that the truck driver with whom I had caught a ride had found my name and address in my wallet and had asked another driver to drop my things off at our home in Bridgedale. The return of my money, clothes, and overnight bag couldn't begin to erase all the feelings I had.

Mr. Farber was surprised to see me. He got up from the bench and walked over to Terry and me.

"Well, well. Just what we need," he said. "Right, Terry? Our regular outfielder. Welcome back, Mickey." Then he looked more serious. "Glad Audrey is all right, and that everything turned out as it did. A lot of us on the team—when we read about the search—wondered if maybe we shouldn't drive up there and help out."

Terry spoke up then. "My Dad and I were getting ready to go when we heard the radio report that Audrey had been found."

"We're playing the Rockets tonight, Mickey," Mr. Farber said. "They've got some long ball hitters on that club, so we'll need your long legs out there in center. We lost to the Yankees, you know."

"Terry told me."

"Is your father here?"

"No. He left on a business trip this morning. He said he might be back for the game, though."

"Again, Mickey, welcome back."

I thanked Mr. Farber; and as he left us then to go back to the bench, Terry and I started to play catch. I wasn't eager to play ball that night, I can tell you. What I felt was guilt. I should have been back with my family in Allens Falls, not here in Bridgedale playing for the Tigers. But I'd ruined Dad's vacation, we'd all come home, and so here I was.

124

Sometimes getting what you want can be just like a punishment.

Anyway, this was an important game. With that loss to the Yankees, the Tigers were in a tie with the Rockets for first place. We really needed this game if we wanted to be in contention by play-off time three more weeks from then.

I started the game in center. It was good to feel the thick grass under my sneakers, and I was anxious to catch a long one. And I got one right away. Like Mr. Farber said, the Rockets had some long ball hitters, and the second batter up swung on the first pitch that Jimmy Kingston threw him and sent a high one into deep center field. I was on my way as soon as the ball hit the bat.

I thought I was going to reach it without any trouble. The ball started to drop, and I slowed and put up my glove. But there was a wind that night—blowing straight out—that I hadn't paid much attention to, and the ball kept drifting farther and farther out. I reached up higher and higher and started to backpedal. And then the ball was past my outstretched glove and bounding against the wooden fence. The batter was fast, and although my throw-in was a good one, he scored standing up.

The next hit to me was after two were out and was a line drive. I played it perfectly, reached up for it, caught it—then immediately dropped it.

Jimmy Kingston struck out the final batter, and I started in. So far, I was *not* covering myself with glory. But this, I told myself, was only the first inning.

We didn't score in our half of the first, and I didn't do anything disgraceful again in the field until the top of the third. The first batter up hit a soft liner over second. I raced in to make a shoestring catch and let the ball get through me. The batter ended up on third, although Terry, who was backing me up, almost cut him down with a fine throw. Jimmy struck out the next batter, and the one after that popped to Dave Parisien, who made a great catch in back of the plate.

Two outs. I hitched up my pants and punched my glove. I wanted the next batter to hit to me—at the same time I didn't. The batter swung. It was a low line drive to my right. I started for it.

Could I get it? If it was my ball, I should call for it—loud and clear. I decided it was my ball.

"I got it! I got it!" I yelled.

The ball was dropping now, and I was going to have to really run to catch it. But for the second time I had forgotten the wind.

126

The ball kept carrying away from me. I lunged, desperately. The balled ticked the end of my glove and bounded past me.

This time it was Bob Lenney who backed me up and threw the ball in.

As I went back to my position, I wasn't sure I wanted the ball hit to me again. I was jinxed. Or at least I was jinxing the Tigers. Luckily, Jimmy struck out the next batter.

I kept my head down while trotting in to the bench. Everyone had been glad to see me back. Well, I was back, all right, but it sure wasn't doing the Tigers any good.

As I slumped down on the bench, Terry patted me on the back to cheer me up. "Never mind, Mickey," he said. "You're just a little rusty, that's all."

I didn't say anything.

Jack Tilson was at bat. That meant I was next. I left the bench, picked up my bat, and moved over to the on-deck circle. The lanky first baseman took the first pitch for a ball, then swung on the next pitch and hit one through the box for a single. I got up and started for the plate.

I represented the tying run. And since I was responsible for both Rocket runs, I felt I had to get a hit, a long one now. The first pitch to me was low and over the plate. I swung. It must have looked as if I

127

were playing golf. I missed the ball by a foot at least.

"Don't be too anxious!" shouted Mr. Farber. "Look them over! Take your time!"

"Make him pitch to you, Mickey!" yelled Terry.

I rubbed some dirt on the handle of the bat and stepped back into the batter's box. They were right. I was swinging at anything. I was trying to make up for my miserable fielding with one mighty blast.

I watched the next pitch go by. It was right over the heart of the plate, belt high for a called strike two. Now the bench was silent. No more advice. I figured with no balls and two strikes, the Rocket pitcher would waste a few. But then, maybe he knew that was what I thought and was deciding to cross me up.

I readied myself and waited for the pitch. It was a fast ball. But it was over the plate. I swung and really got a piece of it. It felt the way it does when you catch the ball on the heavy part of the bat. I lit out for first, my eye on the ball as it soared high and far into center field. It looked as if I had really done it. And then, as I rounded first, I saw the center fielder reach high as he leaned back over the wooden fence and caught the ball.

That was some catch. Maybe I really was jinxed. I trotted back to the bench shaking my head. No matter what I did, it seemed, I was jinxed. I was still feeling guilty, I guess, and there was no way I could shake the feeling.

Mr. Farber slapped me on the shoulder. "Too bad, Mickey. You almost put it out of here."

As I sat down on the bench, I happened to glance up into the stands. My father had arrived along with Audrey and Mom. Then I stopped still and stared. Charlie Johnson was sitting beside my father! When I got over my surprise, I waved to Charlie. He grinned and waved back.

I turned around to watch the game, so excited I could hardly concentrate on what was happening in front of me. Sandy Amaro was at bat. He singled sharply, sending Jack Tilson to third. A moment later Bill Tebo singled, scoring Tilson and sending Sandy to third.

Up stepped Dave Parisien. He was lugging about three or four bats. He swung them around his head a couple of times to loosen up, then tossed all but one of them away.

"Come on, Dave!" I yelled. "Just a little bingle will do it! All we need is a bingle."

But fortunately Dave wasn't listening. He cut on the second pitch to him and sent a long drive into left center. There was no doubt about this one from the moment it left his bat. The Rocket outfielders ran over a way, then watched the ball drop over the low wooden fence.

Four to two, Tigers.

That was all the scoring, and as I trotted out to my position in center field I hoped that my jinx on the team was lifted. I sure didn't feel jinxed anymore, not with Charlie in the stands, and especially knowing that it was my father who had gone and brought him. It would be great to see Charlie again.

Maybe it meant that Dad really wasn't angry deep inside for the way I ruined his vacation. Maybe. I turned around and pounded my glove. My knees suddenly felt weak. I wanted so badly to show Dad and Charlie how good I was so they would understand why I had acted so crazy.

But could I?

10

BUT NOTHING CAME my way in the top of the fourth. Jimmy struck out the first two batters he faced, and Paul Norwood, playing shortstop, made a nice play in the hole and threw out the batter for the third out and a one-two-three inning.

I didn't think I'd get a chance to bat that inning, so I went right on past the bench up into the stands to talk to Charlie.

"You're a sight for sore eyes," I told him. "What are you doing here? Come to shine shoes?"

He laughed. "Nope. Your father found me and asked for a shoeshine. I gave him the best one I could with one hand. And he invited me to Bridgedale to visit you, so I took him up on it. He also mentioned something else, but I'll wait until after the game to discuss it with you." He looked at Dad. "Right, Mr. Ortega?"

My father smiled and nodded. Then he looked at me.

"Go get 'em, Mickey. I understand we need this game."

Then Audrey piped up: "Don't be so nervous, Mickey. Catch all the balls."

My mother laughed. "You're doing fine, Mickey."

I turned and went back to the bench just as the two outs were made.

As I watched, Terry swung on a high pitch and missed by a mile to end the inning.

The top of the fifth was a disaster.

Jimmy had been kind of wild all during the game, but had always managed somehow to get the batter —except, of course, whenever I got involved in the play. So now, in the top of the fifth, he just lost his control completely. He walked the first batter and then the second batter. On the third one he ran the count to three and two. The batter took the next pitch, and it was a ball, high and outside. Dave Parisien had to leap to get it.

Mr. Farber came out then. He spoke to Jimmy for a short time, then motioned to Paul Norwood to come in to the mound and pitch. Jimmy slapped the ball down into Paul's glove as he passed him on his way to shortstop. While Paul warmed up, Jimmy practiced the long throw from deep short.

I walked over to right field to talk to Terry.

"You want me to take anything that comes close?" Terry asked.

I thought a moment. "No," I said. "Anything I can get to, I'll take."

"Okay. I'll back you up."

"You've been doing just fine, so far. I guess I need a bushel basket."

Terry didn't reply, and I walked back to my position. He was only trying to help by offering to go after any balls that I might not feel up to reaching, but I was a center fielder. It was my job to range the farthest, to take any questionable balls. That was because I was supposed to be the fastest outfielder, and the one with the surest hands. I punched my glove. Well, if that was what I was supposed to be, that was what I would be.

Paul Norwood was ready to pitch. He turned to look back at us in the outfield to make sure we were in position. Then he faced the fourth Rocket batter of the inning and struck him out on three blazing fast balls.

I relaxed.

I shouldn't have. The next batter swung on Paul's second fast ball and sent it on a line into deep left center. I turned and raced for the fence, looking back over my shoulder at the ball. It was no longer rising, but it was still coming. I increased my speed and stuck my glove up, hoping it was in the path of the ball. I was more lucky than anything else, I suppose, when the ball slammed into the pocket of my glove and stayed there.

That was when I looked around. I was just in time to see the fence coming at me. I put out both hands to cushion the impact. But even so, the momentum of my run kept me going, and I toppled headfirst over the fence and landed sitting up in a mess of golden-rod. I sat there, dazed for a moment, until I heard Terry and Bob Lenney's running footsteps approaching from the other side of the fence. I jumped up then and tossed the nearest of them the ball. That was Bob Lenney. He whirled and gunned a throw-in.

The three runners had been off at the crack of the bat and were surprised at my catch and had to race back to tag up. The fellow on third did also, but he was still able to make it home before I recovered my senses and tossed the ball to Bob. And the other two runners moved up one base also.

Men on second and third, two outs, one run already in.

I got all kinds of cheers for that catch, but I couldn't see where it had done much good. I was certain of it a moment later when a scratch single up the middle scored two more runs to make it five to four, Rockets in the lead again.

The next batter hit a soft liner to Bob Lenney in left. He came in fast and caught the ball just above his shoe tops to end the inning.

Jimmy Kingston led off in the bottom of the fifth. I guess he was upset about how he had pitched. He looked that way, anyway. He stood there in the batter's box, waving his bat menacingly at the pitcher. The first pitch to him was low, but we could all see him straining not to go for it. Then he looked up at the sky, turned and left the batter's box, grabbed a handful of dirt, and rubbed it on his hands and on the handle of the bat. All the while he was doing this, he was glaring out at the pitcher, as if he wanted to clobber him or something. He stepped back into the batter's box and waited. The pitch came in a little high, but Jimmy couldn't restrain himself and swung. The ball went right past the pitcher's glove on a line, and Jimmy was on first with a lead-off single.

We all came to life then, jumping up and yelling encouragement as Bob Lenney approached the batter's box.

But Bob struck out. Terry Lawson was luckier. He walked. So that meant two men on, one out.

Now it was Jack Tilson's turn. He worked the count to three and two and began fouling off pitches like mad. And then he walked.

Bases were loaded, and it was my turn to bat.

As I left the on-deck circle and headed for the plate, I wanted to glance back at the stands because I could feel Charlie's eyes and my father's eyes on the back of my neck. I wasn't worried about a scout anymore, but I surely wanted this opportunity to show them that there was something to my ambition to make professional baseball a career.

And I also wanted the Tigers to win.

I guess all of this made me a little nervous. My fingers were so sweaty around the handle of the bat that I didn't even offer at the first pitch, which was right over the plate for a called strike. Still standing in the batter's box, I reached down and grabbed a handful of dirt and rubbed it briskly into my palms.

"Hands feel kind of sweaty, don't they?" said the catcher, grinning at me through the bars of his mask. "I wouldn't worry if I were you. There's no chance of your getting a hit."

His remarks didn't bother me—until the next pitch. That one, too, was right over, and I swung on it as hard as I could and missed completely. Strike two.

I stepped out of the batter's box. I was scared. I could see myself walking back from the plate after striking out with everyone looking away and a few of the guys saying, "That's all right, Mickey." But I squared my shoulders and stepped back into the batter's box.

The next pitch was inside. I swung on it, caught the ball on the handle of the bat, but pulled it foul down the left field line. It was a mean smash, and the people in the left field stands had to really scramble to get out of the way. Although it was only a foul ball, it was the first time in a long time I had swung that hard and felt that nice, clean impact that carries clear up to your shoulders when you catch a ball just right.

The next pitch was outside, and I let it go by for a ball.

"That's the old eye," called Mr. Farber from the bench.

I looked at him and nodded slightly. My throat was too dry for me to say anything.

The next pitch came in low and outside. I almost went after it, but held up in time. I stepped out of the batter's box and looked out at the pitcher. As I

137

rubbed some more dirt on the handle of my bat, I did some thinking. He had two strikes on me, and I must have looked like an easy out for him. Now he had two balls as well as two strikes. He wouldn't want to waste another pitch, because then he would be pitching with the bases loaded and the count three and two. So maybe, I thought, he just might put this one over.

I stepped back in the batter's box, looking for a fast ball over the plate. The pitcher went into his windup and came around with the ball. It was about letter high and fast as blazes. I had guessed right. I swung. The clean crack of the bat told me I had gotten good wood on the ball as I dropped my bat and raced for first. The ball landed between the left and center fielders. The center fielder made a nice backhand stop and fired the ball in to the second baseman. I was more than halfway to second base, and I could see the play was going to be close. I had to slide. A few feet from the bag I threw myself feetfirst at second base and slid across the bag an instant before the second baseman's glove slapped down onto my foot.

The umpire was right on the play and called me safe. I got up, brushing my uniform off, and looked around at the empty bases. With those three runs, we were now ahead seven to five.

Sandy Amaro was up. On the second pitch, he hit a short fly into center. The center fielder ran in, reached up, and missed the ball. The moment the ball touched his glove, I was off for third. Luckily, the throw from the center fielder was wide, and I slid in under the tag. Now I was beginning to feel like a ballplayer again as I got up and brushed off my uniform.

Bill Tebo stepped up to the plate and didn't waste any time at all. He swung on the first pitch and topped a roller out toward the mound. I was off the moment he swung, racing down the baseline for home. I didn't see the pitcher pick up the ball, but I saw the catcher reaching high, a look of surprise on his face. Then I saw the ball glance off the top of his mitt and head for the backstop. I didn't bother to slide as I scored with the eighth run.

As I trotted to the bench, I got quite a reception. I must admit I felt pretty good. I felt so good I waved to Charlie and Dad.

We didn't score any more runs after that. Dave Parisien and Paul Norwood struck out. In the top of the sixth, Paul had little trouble with the

Rocket batters, and the game ended with the score Rockets five, Tigers eight.

My father was talking to Mr. Farber when I broke away from the rest of the players and started toward him. Dad smiled at me as I approached, then looked at Mr. Farber.

"I'm sure Mickey wishes he could play the next couple of weeks, but I don't think he'll be wanting to. I'm hoping Mickey and the rest of the family—as well as a special friend of his—can return to the mountains and finish the vacation we started a week ago. We still have two weeks left."

He looked at me then. "What do you think, Mickey?"

"I think that's a great idea. Is that what Charlie meant?"

Dad nodded.

Mr. Farber smiled, stepped closer to me, and placed a strong hand on my shoulder. "That sounds like a fine idea, Mickey. I've got a hunch we're going to make the play-offs. You should be back in plenty of time for them."

I said good-bye to him then and went back to the car with my Dad. It was so great to see Charlie again.

I asked him about his mother and his brothers and sisters. He said that they were fine and that his mother had insisted that he take the vacation.

Once we were in the car, my father looked around at the rest of us. "Okay, gang. Here we go again. Tomorrow morning we drive back to the lake." He started the car and pulled away from the curb.

As we drove home with Audrey on one side of me and Charlie on the other, I realized how lucky I was. We were a family again, and I was part of it. Maybe someday I would play Major League baseball, but I had learned from Charlie and from almost losing Audrey how important my family was to me. And my Dad, too. And that, I now realized, was even more important than becoming a big league ballplayer.

Meanwhile, Charlie and I were going back to the lake with all the whippoorwills and the mist in the early morning hours and then maybe—just maybe— a return to Bridgedale and a chance to close the season out in center field for the Tigers, loping after those high fly balls to center field.